Oh Crumbs!

and other
Short Stories in support of the

British Deaf Association

Alison Lingwood

Contents

Foreword

Oh Crumbs!

Sox and the Chox

Underneath the Arches

The Mawkin

I Couldn't give a Cluck

Lovely Lizzie

Last Bus to Wareham

The Fungarium

The Prophet of Doom

Splash

Scooters for All

Don't Mess with the Bride

The Junk Drawer

The Pan Gremlins

Caroline's Cart

The Coffee Bean

Hole in One

First Date

The Switch

Clippety Clop

The Best Friend's Guilt Trip

All Change at Number Twelve

Where has James Gone?

Otto

Unlucky for Some

Green Beans and Baby Carrots

Agony or Ecstasy

Three Strikes and You're Out

An Advisory Tale

The Book List

Bangers, No Mash

A Truly Delightful Gentleman

The Best Present

Acknowledgements

Foreword

Estimates suggest that there are over 150,000 UK users of British Sign Language, over 87,000 of whom are deaf. This figure discounts professionals working in the field.

All proceeds from my four volumes:

The Hairdryer died Today
Mission Accomplished!
Wedding Wings
Oh Crumbs!

are donated to the British Deaf Association, to further their work into promotion, education and information about BSL and other ways to support the deaf community. I hope that you will enjoy the stories and spread the word to your family and friends.

To find out more about the work of the British Deaf Association contact **bda@bda.org.uk** or 07795 410724

Oh Crumbs!

Now I'm not really one to criticise someone else's housekeeping style; I've seen and heard some weird things in this household though, like the other week when the youngest of the children shook out the contents of a finished bread bag in order to use the bag for something. It was a mixed grain loaf and his mother Clare went running into the living area shouting that there was an infestation of some sort in the kitchen, they were all over the floor. On closer inspection her husband announced that they were the wheatgerm and seed bits from the loaf. It had been one of those that boasted five different seeds and grains, very tasty I'm sure but the young boy's mother nearly had a fit when they were scattered all over the floor. I think she thought they were mouse droppings – ugh!

In fact what she refers to as the *kitchen* is really just one end of this big room. The whole family calls it that, and they call the other bit the *living room*. As it is, it's just one big open space.

We, my friends and I, are in the bin – that's

what it's called, the bread bin. It doesn't sound very nice in my opinion, rather like the thing under the sink that they put rubbish in, and that gets a bit whiffy sometimes, especially in the warm weather, but we'll gloss over that. Anyway, the bread bin is one of those shiny silvery ones with a lid that rolls forward when it closes, the idea being to look tidy and also to keep the bread inside fresh. I think sometimes this family is a little bit optimistic about how much bread will fit in here, hence the occasion when my heel got shoved up against the hinge mechanism, where I've been stuck ever since.

They do seem to get through loads of different bread though, and sometimes they cram so much in that we're all pushed out of shape. I've seen all sorts in here, all shapes and sizes and of course all colours; pale, lily-white, right through golden to a really dark brown. Even bluey-green occasionally, like I am now. The colour doesn't matter though; you shouldn't judge a book by its cover, or in this case a loaf by its crust.

It's not that Clare doesn't clean the bread bin, I wouldn't want you to think that. If she could see the inside when the lid is closed, which of course she can't, then she'd spot me easily. But as she opens the bin, the hinge mechanism hides me completely. So here I remain, watching all the comings and goings.

I consider myself quite exotic in comparison to some of the others who pass through here. I've been here since just before last Christmas; that's why I mentioned housekeeping skills. To be fair I am very tiny and I'm stuck – that's how come I've been here long enough to go mouldy, and to see all the bready traffic that I have. It's a very eclectic household this, and that's why I'm so reluctant to free myself from in this awkward hinge. I love to see the changes in the bin. I'm the heel of a stollen loaf bought in for last Christmas. Fortunately all the marzipan from my middle and the icing sugar from on top of me got eaten and, as so often happens with breads after a few days, nobody wanted the drier bit at the end. There was still no reason to slam my foot in the hinge in my opinion, but here we are. I was determined not to let our relationship crumble, I like living here, and we have fun.

   The bread bin's position on the counter means that I can just see the calendar hanging on the kitchen wall and so I know that it's May now. The family all seem to be talking about something called Eurovision and there are all sorts of foreigners in here at the moment. Now, don't get me wrong, I like variety as much as the next crumb, and obviously I'm from Germany myself, though via that little bakery on the High Street. Some of them though would try the patience of a saint. We had one in here at the beginning of this week, all gone now thank goodness. Didn't she think she was something special? She announced herself as a *Pain au Chocolat*; she certainly got the *pain* bit right, but of course she pronounced it in the French way, very *chic*! Bleugh!

   We've had a variety of French breads and cakes in here before, and some have been very nice. Even now there's a bit of leftover baguette, who we call CDG. That stands for Charles de Gaulle, who was a French President, so he tells us. There's only a few centimetres of him left now. He too has suffered the fate I was telling you about before; he's just the hard bit at the end, which always gets left. It's a frequent occurrence with baguettes, he says. Apparently the end of a baguette is just the same shape as the real Charles de Gaulle's nose in profile, hence the nickname. He doesn't mind us calling him that, in fact he made the joke in the first place. He's a bit of a lad, to be honest; he's got his eye on some crumpet at the back of the bin at the moment. I need to keep a close watch on him! Good job there are no bloomers in here just now.

He's very cheerful though, not like a guy we had in here a month or so ago, he was a real sour dough. CDG is down to earth too, not like this week's *Pain* at all! Talk about stuck up, proper upper crust she thought herself. And that's another thing, she was really sticky. The chocolate had begun to soften in this toasty weather we've been having and I thought we were all going to end up covered in chocolate, whether we liked it or not. That's okay if you're meant to be like that but some of us are definitely meant to be savoury, and chocolate doesn't really work. Anyway it seems that she tasted very sweet and so she quickly got eaten; she didn't even make it to Eurovision night. I wonder how she'd feel if she knew that she'd been replaced by a small plastic bag of croutons.

Listening to the family's conversation Eurovision night works like this, they each pick a name out of a hat at random; the name of a country that takes part in this singing competition. They colour in a paper flag for that country, and bring some of the appropriate food and drink to share on the night. I don't know anything about the drink, but there are two different types of bread from each country. That is crackers, and it's the reason why the bin's so stuffed at the moment; stuffed fuller than I was with marzipan in my early days. The *pain*'s gone so I guess the French entry is going to be indicated by the croutons I told you about, and a couple of croissants over there.

Clare's husband's selection was Israel, so we have some beautifully glazed bagels in the bin. We also have matzo, the unleavened bread from there. In fact there's often matzo here in the bin, since the family discovered a liking for it back in April, when it was Passover. This year the Jewish festival coincided with Easter, so there were spicy hot cross buns around then too. They smelled yummy. None of us in here eats bread of course, that would be cannibalism, but we can sure appreciate the various aromas.

Italy must have been a tough call, there are so many lovely breads from there. At the moment I can see some ciabatta, who was getting a bit above himself to be honest, until CDG, who is very well educated, slapped him down. He told the ciabatta that it was only invented in 1982 by a baker in the Italian province of Adria, to try to compete with the popularity of baguettes. Crumbs! That went against the grain and the ciabatta got a right cob on! But it's all calm in here again now. Much more sweet and mellow is the other Italian offering of panettone from Milan. I must say it seems a bit of a mish-mash to me, lemon and orange rind, cherries, raisins and booze. It smells a bit like a pub in here, but she's a pleasant enough young lady.

Oh, here we go. The family is loafing around in front of the television now. They've taken the breads they want out of the bin, and left the lid open, so I've got a really good view. They leave the UK out of the equation apparently, so everyone has to go for something a little different, and I got quite put off my train of thought when I saw Clare pop some of my lovely new friends into the toaster! The toaster! From there they've come out partly incinerated and I got quite upset and shouted, '*Oh no, he's toast!*' but then CDG pointed out that some of the chaps in here are barely palatable unless they're in that state, so I suppose it's okay.

The one who got toasted was a bit of a weird fellow anyway – a sandwich short of a picnic, I think. It was just a bit alarming to watch those we'd been chatting to a few moments before, although it has certainly improved the smell of some of them, and they're all going to get eaten anyway.

In my momentary panic about the toaster I nearly forgot to tell you about Germany's offerings, which Clare herself has drawn this year. She's gone for some pumpernickel bread, which is dark and sweet in a treacly sort of way. Her second offering is pretzels. I love pretzels, the shape of them is so cute, like a little knot or a smiley face. They're savoury, salted and crunchy, so they tell me. It looks like the family love them too, there aren't many left and the programme has only just started. Here we go, let's get ready to crumble!

Well, Eurovision was last night, and a great time was had by all in the household, although I think they're going to need their five a day for a week or so to clear out all the carbohydrates they've eaten. A lot of the hilarity was as a result of what they brought in to drink I suspect, but they definitely had fun. And so to the results: the competition on the television was won by Sweden whom nobody here had chosen, but Israel came third, so Clare's husband was the winner in the family. Then Italy came fourth, which one of the youngsters had chosen, so he was very smug.

For the rest of the family though, this year's Eurovision scores *nul points*.

It had gone very quiet here in the bin once the Eurovision excitement was over. Until today, I heard the family chatting, whilst Clare's husband was out. It seems that this year his birthday and something called Fathers' Day coincide on a date next month, and they're having a party – yeah! A party is bound to include us here in the bin, isn't it? Clare's cleaned the bin out since Eurovision, but I'm still here, so hopefully I'll still be around for this party. They're talking about maybe burgers in buns, sausage rolls, birthday cake and snacks – breadsticks, and perhaps pretzels, they didn't last long last time.

It's been a bit dull in here since Eurovision, but now we're planning for a party, that's exciting!

I think a bit of excitement is what we all … *knead.*

Sox and the Chox

In the nineteen fifties the danger to dogs that lies in their consumption of chocolate was not understood, or certainly not as well as it is now.

A young teenage boy, not very sociable, not very outgoing, with no particular hobbies other than listening to music on the radio, was difficult to buy presents for. Chocolates, only milk chocolates and of a particular brand, let's call them Mairy Dilk, were always sure fire winners though, and so it was that for one particular birthday he received two half pound slabs of chocolate, and also two one pound boxes of, let's call it Trilk May. Quite a haul for a young lad!

In the family lived a small dog with very short legs. He was called Sox, because he was brown with white paws. He was seldom left on his own but on this particular occasion, for reasons now long forgotten, the family had to leave him behind. They left the house mid-afternoon and would not return until late at night. It was not very long that the dog would be alone, but longer than usual.

Returning after an enjoyable afternoon and a

convivial evening, they found that the dog was not in his usual place in the window waiting for them. He heard them though, heard them approaching the house and as they opened the front door he appeared round the corner of the stairs.

Sox was not allowed to go upstairs, and ordinarily would never go up unless given express permission. Clearly when he was left alone his doggy brain felt that the usual rules didn't apply. Having made a fuss of the dog, and letting him out, the lady of the house went upstairs and found a warm patch in the middle of the bed in the master bedroom. The little dog had evidently decided that this was a reasonable place to wait out his ordeal, however long it proved to be.

There were other clues to his anxiety. Their son's chocolate presents had been on the shelf in his bedroom and Sox had found them. He must have spent the missing hours unwrapping the purple and silver wrappers off the bars of chocolate; the contents had disappeared completely. The wrappers were scattered all over his bedroom floor, as was the cellophane wrapping from round the two chocolate boxes.

There seemed at first to be no evidence of the chocolate whatsoever. Although, on further examination ... under the sideboard in the dining room were a couple of items that further incriminated the little dog. One of the selection of flavours in the assortment boxes was *Coconut Ice*, which for some reason was wrapped individually in fancy silver and purple foil. Clearly a dog of discernment (in my opinion) Sox had sampled the range of chocolates on offer, including ripping the wrapping paper off said coconut ice chocolates. These he had rejected. They had been painstakingly unwrapped, and the contents unceremoniously spat out on the carpet.

In the boxes of Trilk May, the consumer was offered two examples of each filling, including the Coconut Ice. Undeterred by his dislike of the first of these, Sox had carried on, unwrapping and then also spitting out the second one, before moving on and doing the same with the second box.

Thankfully he was unharmed by the massive consumption of chocolate he imbibed that day, but I have to say that, as someone with a strong dislike of desiccated coconut myself, he went up hugely in my estimation of his good taste.

Underneath the Arches

It had been a pure whim and having an hour to spare that led to Izzy finding the shop at all. Visiting the town where she was brought up in a fit of nostalgia, she saw that The Pack Horse Inn had closed down. The only pub that she had ever been asked to leave aged fifteen, when she and a friend had dared each other to ask for a shandy at the bar.

Looking through the archway, where the packhorses and their carts used to be driven across the cobbles to the stables in days gone by, she saw the To Let sign and went to explore. The front part of the old pub was now a smart clothes shop, and the empty unit was accessed under the arch, where the laden pack horses used to be stabled. On the left side, behind the dress shop, there were two doors, one a regular wooden door leading to the empty unit, and, next to it, a stable door, leading to what had originally been the first of several loose boxes. Looking through the grimy door she could see that the two had been knocked through.

Izzy had a sudden image as she stood there on

the cobbles of how this could be; two adjacent doors – one full sized and the other the same style but child-sized. The stable door would be easy to convert; she could secure the top half so that only the lower door would open. This was how she had imagined the front of the book shop she had always dreamed of owning.

An old hatch provided the possibility too of a little window low down next to the stable door, where she could stand the metre high cardboard cut-out of Peter Rabbit that had followed her from one home to another. It had cluttered up her various bedrooms since she first spotted it in the window of a children's clothing shop that was closing down. Standing there on the cobbles, she had immediately arranged a viewing, and within a few days had arranged to take the lease of the two adjoining units.

The viewings had taken place in the afternoons and, the first time she arrived before ten in the morning, laden with boxes and painting equipment, she had been alarmed to find a group of three men sleeping on her doorstep. The doors were sheltered by the archway and a decision had to be made as they stood warily before her. As she was inside, turning on lights and filling her new kettle, they had wandered off. Perhaps that was the last she would see of them, now they knew that the shop was no longer empty.

What she hadn't expected over the next few mornings, was to find the three rough sleepers stretched out on the doorstep and the cobbles each time she arrived.

The third morning was really cold, and she made a spontaneous decision. Instead of threatening them or calling the police, she looked around. There really was nothing they could harm here. They were hardly likely to break into a bookshop, and may they could even offer some protection.

'Hi guys! If you let me get inside I'll get the kettle on and I'll bring you out a hot cuppa, it's a bit chilly out here. What do you say?'

There were a few incoherent grunts and the men shuffled to one side.

Putting the kettle on and digging out mugs from under the ancient sink, she went back to find that one of the men had wandered off, whilst the other two had carried in the two boxes of books she had left under the archway.

Over time Izzy came to see this little group – the two regulars, Ted and Joey, and various odd other individuals who came and went – as her helpers. Over those first few days she set ground rules. Any indication of drugs or alcohol and they would not be welcome, and no begging off customers in or around the shop. She started the morning by dispensing tea or hot soup from a panful made the previous evening, or a dish of cereal if they preferred. She also enlisted their help in washing up after themselves, and cleaning up the area immediately outside the shop. She surprised herself by how tough she could be; only occasionally did she have to threaten to close up and leave them to it.

To Izzy's alarm after she had been there a couple of months the landlord told her that he intended to install a gate at the end of archways, adjacent to the footpath. Two further units had now been let beyond hers, a café and a craft shop. The landlord felt that they would be safer if they were locked up at night. Izzy persuaded him that the little group of men, led by Ted, made excellent watchdogs, reminding him that they had sounded the alarm when there had been a fire in the kitchen at the back of the clothes shop, thus preventing a disaster. She and the café owner kept a copy of each other's door key and telephone number, as a back-up.

Now she approached the bright wooden door, painted pillar box red, with a similar but child-sized sunshine yellow door immediately next to it, where children could let themselves into and out of the shop.

On the outside of the shop, to the left of the full-sized door were two trestle tables, where inexpensive paperbacks were displayed. These she covered over each night, and she suspected that Ted and Joey slept underneath them.

Next to the children's door was the window, again at child height, with the cardboard cut-out of Peter Rabbit peeping out around a chintz curtain. The children's door led into the children's area where everything was scaled down. Comfy little sofas lined the far wall, and a chest-high solid barrier immediately to the right gave an illusion of seclusion from the adults. The shop was divided into zones, each with its own flavour. The small children's zone was themed around Peter Rabbit with ornaments on a high shelf, the only thing out of reach of small fingers, but these had been a gift from Izzy's grandmother. She was happy to share them, but didn't want them broken, they were too precious.

There was a section for slightly older children, with an old rowing boat in the middle. Izzy had bought the damaged boat cheaply and had it firmly fixed to the shop floor. Children could climb into the boat to sit and read. To complete The Owl and the Pussycat theme the boat was painted green, there was a huge painted owl peeping over the doorway, and a cat was painted on the opposite wall, before an American diner-style area for the older ones.

On quiet days, which were frequent, she would sit and chat with Ted and Joey, who seldom spoke, but whom she learned was Ted's brother. She never enquired as to the nature of Joey's disability. He was a hard worker but needed constant supervision. Every morning he would polish the door fittings with the brass polish Izzy provided, but he would do one only. Then he needed specifically to be told to do the second door. It happened every day, and he never managed to take the initiative for himself. Sometimes Izzy arrived in the morning to find that Ted and Joey had already left the archway, and it might be several days before she saw them. They always slept there though, and if they left early in the morning there was still the evidence that they had swept the cobbles outside the shop, and Joey would have polished the doorknobs and letterboxes as usual. She didn't feel it was appropriate to ask where they went, and even less so to ask what they did. There were never any problems when they were around, in fact a couple of times they saw off youngsters who were out looking for a bit of mischief at a shopkeeper's expense.

As time passed it was the mundane, run of the mill books that kept the shop going. Books that often could have been bought more cheaply at the supermarket, but there was a growing band of stoical readers who seemed determined to keep the little independent bookshop alive.

Izzy was able to employ a Saturday girl, a keen reader herself, who would hunt through markets and charity shops, and scour social media both for stock and for artefacts. She had a real flair for display, and proved invaluable.

Since opening the shop nearly five years ago, there had been highs and lows, but the former far outweighed the latter. There were lows such as a flood, when Izzy's little team of helpers had been so helpful. A leak in the roof had led to water pouring into the shop and a considerable amount of stock had been damaged. Ted, Joey and one of their friends had helped rescue and dry as many of the books as they could, and, once everything was dry enough, they had helped Izzy to repaint the shop.

The lows were overwhelmed by some real high points, and Izzy always looked forward to unpacking a new box of books, never sure what treasures it might hold. On one such occasion a box of books had been dumped outside the shop overnight. Ted could tell her little about the person who left it, other than that he was a middle aged man. Most of the books were paperbacks, a couple of series of adventure stories, which she displayed on the trestle tables outside the door, covered over at night with sheets of plastic. At the bottom of the box was one red-bound hardback volume. It was nothing special, a Readers' Digest collection of short stories, but had been nicely bound in its day. Fastened to it with a couple of elastic bands was a white autograph book. As the shop was quite busy that day she put the two together on the shelf and forgot about them.

Until she heard a woman crying. A woman had been casually browsing through the shelves when she suddenly burst into tears. Taking a detour via the kettle – a hot drink often helped – Izzy went to the woman who was holding the battered white autograph book.

The tears, it turned out, were of happiness or nostalgia. The woman had looked at the inscription on the first page: *Wee Donal' 1959.* Without looking further she handed the book to Izzy and faultlessly recited the writing on the last page: *By hook or by crook I'll be last in this book, Stella.* Underneath, in tiny writing was scribed: *Sez you Sis, Bernie.*

'Stella was my Mum, and her brother was Bernard, Uncle Bernie. This was my Dad's book. I remember it so well. See here, where the white writing that says *Autographs* is picked off? I did that. I remember my dad being so cross, and explaining that we didn't deface books ever. We didn't have that many books when I was little and this was always on the shelf in the living room. When we lost my dad, Mum was ruthless about throwing all his stuff out, she wouldn't countenance us keeping any mementos. I came home from school one day and everything had gone.

'Let me see if I can remember my favourite one:

A friend that is new is all that is true, but there's never a friend like the old.

The former is held by a silver thread, the latter by anchors of gold.'

As the woman spoke, Izzy flicked through the book. There was the verse, just as the woman had remembered it. It was a learning point for her, not to assume that any book was worthless. She wished the lady luck in tracking where the autograph book had been in the meantime, and gifted it to her. The lady returned again and again, bringing her family and seldom leaving without buying a couple of books.

* * *

Then the unthinkable happened, and Izzy fell ill. She closed the shop on a Friday evening, feeling fine, and then on the Saturday morning she was stuck in bed and unable to go out for over a week. She telephoned the café owner, who agreed to put a sign in the window at *Underneath the Arches*. She promised also to let Ted and Joey know what had happened.

When Izzy turned onto the cobbles a week the following Monday, she was alarmed to see that the shop lights were on, the paperback trestles outside the door were uncovered, and the front door to the shop stood open. She approached tentatively, not sure what to expect. There was no notice on the door, and she could hear voices.

'She might be well enough to come back.' It was unmistakably Ted, 'Go to the shop on the corner and get some milk. If Izzy's able to come into the shop the first thing she'll want is a cuppa.'

'You're right there,' Izzy found Ted behind the counter, handing over some money to Joey.

'Thank goodness you're back. People kept coming and wanting to buy the books, so I borrowed the key from the café, and we've been really busy. I'll be glad to give you the key back though, it's too much responsibility for me, this. I just didn't want you to lose out because you weren't here.

'I've written down everything we've sold and the amount. I didn't know what to do with the money though, so I put it in a bag and used it as a pillow. I had to tell people that they could only pay cash until you were back, and two people dropped off boxes of books to sell. They will call in later this week, to see if you're around.'

'You are miracle workers. Here Joey,' she handed over some more money, 'As well as the milk, get some cream cakes for the three of us for with our drink. I need to keep my strength up.'

Izzy returned the key to the café, where she learned that Ted and Joey had consulted the owner about what they planned to do. She said that it was sweet, they were so worried about Izzy losing customers; they had worked really hard.

That evening, Izzy stood outside the shop, the books covered over and the doors closed. She had wanted to pay Ted and Joey, but they refused, saying she did enough for them already. Ted said that she had given them so much, not treated them like pariahs, but given them their dignity without crowding them or criticizing their lifestyle.

She looked at the now darkened windows, and at the two men settling down under the trestle tables for the night.

It had been the outside of the shop, with its possibilities, that had first attracted Izzy to the premises in what used to be The Pack Horse Inn. It had been the possibility of the little children's door adjacent to the normal one; it had been the motley group of rough sleepers who had now become her helpers and her friends.

The Mawkin

It was the hat that made Tasha bend down and take a good look; a straw hat with multi coloured felt flowers adorning a red band. But I'm getting ahead of myself.

The lane was narrow from the motorway into the small town, but Tasha could drive it almost with her eyes closed. Since moving to the area just six months ago she drove it every morning and reversed the journey every afternoon at five o'clock when she left the office.

As she drove on this particular morning she peered more closely through the window as the coach in front of her seemed to be moving erratically across the narrow lanes in the rain. Instinctively her foot lifted off the accelerator and hovered over the brake. She switched the windscreen wipers to their highest setting as another cloudburst swept in from the south. The coach seemed to right itself as it approached the pub on the left side of the road, and Tasha smiled to herself, as she did most mornings, at its name: *The Mawkin and Firkin*. Once again she promised herself she would look up the meaning, but once again she wouldn't do so. She had a vague idea that a firkin may be an old-fashioned term for a barrel, but she had no idea what a mawkin might be.

It was a strangely positioned pub, with the car park reached first on the left, then the building itself was end on to the road, fronting onto the car park. Beyond the building lay the pub garden, with its scattered tables and chairs, and a gazebo, shielded from the road by a hedge.

Tasha's car reached the entrance to the car park as the coach again veered across to face oncoming traffic, if there was any; the position and size of the coach made it impossible for Tasha to see. Then describing a wide arc the large vehicle swept across in front of her, just beyond the pub building, where it bounced up onto the kerb and crashed through the hedge into the pub garden. It teetered for a second, then settled back on its wheels, remaining upright. There seemed a moment of silence when nothing happened, then the gazebo slowly leaned over to the side under the coach's attack, and collapsed in a heap of wood as if it was sinking to its knees.

Tasha flung her car left into the car park and the car behind followed her. She was vaguely aware of a middle-aged woman in a business suit, as the two women ran to the driver's door of the coach. The driver was conscious and trying to open the door. The coach engine had stalled, but the windscreen wipers still swept impotently across the pebbledash patterns on the broken glass.

The two women looked at each other in horror, then the middle-aged woman pulled out her phone to call the emergency services. The driver was shaken, but conscious and kept telling them he was okay. Tasha thought that she had better check the front of the coach. It was very unlikely that anyone had been in the gazebo or in a pub garden before nine o'clock on a weekday morning, but once the idea was in her head, she needed to make sure.

And it was as she pulled up her jacket hood against the rain, and rounded the front of the coach that she saw the hat, a woman's hat, lying in the grass right in front of the collapsed gazebo. Her heart skipped a beat. What would a hat being doing there, other than being worn on somebody's head? But there was no sign of anyone, and no sound other than of the phone call being made behind her.

She bent down until her face was nearly brushing the top of the wet grass, and peered under the coach. Suddenly she felt sick. There was a shape; almost certainly a human shape flattened under the centre of the coach. Somebody must have been standing in the garden, and been mown down by the large vehicle. She stretched out her hand, but the figure was too central under the hot metalwork for Tasha to be able to reach.

'There's a second person,' she called to the other woman, whose eyes widened in horror, 'under the coach.'

The information was passed on down the phone and the two women sat on the nearest pub garden chairs to wait. They had persuaded the coach driver not to move until someone arrived to check him over. Tasha felt sick; it had been such a shock. She laid her head down on her arms across the table.

It seemed forever but was only a matter of a few minutes before the police arrived, followed almost immediately by two ambulances.

'Where's the second patient?' one of the ambulance drivers asked, looking around.

'Under the coach,' Tasha's voice was little more than a squeak. The paramedics looked at each other. Two of them went round the far side of the coach, whilst the crew from the other ambulance went to help the driver out of his vehicle.

'We need the lifting gear. I can't reach,' Tasha heard one of them say, 'not even to check for a pulse, but there's no sign of movement, nor are they answering when I speak.'

It seemed to take forever before a crane was positioned over the coach so that it could be moved out of the way. The coach driver was on his way to hospital, the second ambulance crew standing by. Tasha and the other lady had been asked to wait at the other side of the garden, their statements would be required. The pub landlord, disturbed by all the noise, opened up the bar, and took them inside to dry off and wait. He brought them each a glass of brandy, and seated them at the table furthest from the window onto the activity. Tasha and her companion from the other car, sipped the restorative drinks, and fought to control their nausea.

The lift seemed to be very slow, with adjustments every few minutes, to haul up the front of the coach, without doing any further damage to the figure underneath. The procedure was paused as soon as there was space for one of the paramedics to slide under to check over the victim. He slid out again almost immediately, trying to hide a smile of relief.

'It's a mawkin,' he told his companion, who shook his head and laughed and immediately shared the news on his radio, 'We're standing down, it's just a mawkin.' He made his way inside to where the two women were sitting.

'Not surprised that sight scared you, looking under the coach, but it's just a mawkin,' he told the ladies and the publican, with a grin of relief, 'That's all. Thank goodness. Quite the coincidence, eh?' He nodded towards the pub sign and at last Tasha found her voice, 'I often wonder as I pass, but I'm not sure what you mean. I'm not local to the area. What is a mawkin?'

The landlord explained, 'It's the local word for a scarecrow. This weekend will be the annual scarecrow festival in the town. All the businesses and a lot of the houses have them and there are competitions.'

He was still talking but Tasha had zoned out. A scarecrow! Not a person. Thank goodness. Not a grisly corpse mown down by an erratically driven coach, just a pile of clothes and the fancy hat, dressed up as a scarecrow for a celebration weekend.

A mawkin. It was just a mawkin.

I Couldn't give a Cluck

Things have suddenly changed in here. In the past the lights were never dimmed, it was always warm, and a constant conveyor belt passed before us, with food and water. There wasn't much of it but we could just help ourselves. Now the conveyor belt stands idle, and the open pipe where water used to trickle, has dried up. The lights have gone out too.

Supposedly if it's always warm and 'daylight' we will all be fooled into thinking that every day's a sunny summer's day, even when it's winter and night-time, and we will go on and on laying an egg every day until we die. That is the plan.

I don't know why there has been this sudden change, but it doesn't bode well. I can't turn round, none of us can. We can only see our next door neighbours, left and right. There are rows and rows of us, many thousands. Each of the battery cages I have heard is as big as a sheet of A4 paper. I don't know what that is, being a hen, but I know there's no space for me to turn round, or stretch my wings, I just sit here day after day popping out eggs, which are immediately whisked away somewhere. There's nothing to do in the dark now but sleep, but I'm getting very hungry and even more thirsty.

Whoa! Just a minute, something's happening! All the lights are suddenly on again, and there's noise, a lot of loud noise. Not the relentless hum of machinery that kept food and water coming, but a big vehicle has reversed through the double doors, and seems to be waiting for something.

Now we're all being picked up, well maybe not all, but quite a lot of us. We're being checked over. Some of the girls are injured, but most of the people handling us seem to be very gentle.

Apparently there's a gap of a few feet at the base of all the wall panels of the massive shed where I've been living, to let in the fresh air but I haven't ever been able to reach it. Reach it! I couldn't even see it. It's only now that I've been lifted up and put in this big vehicle, that I was briefly able to see the sky, and feel the wind and rain on my feathers. Not that I have that many feathers. Looking around quite a few of us look really bald. I suppose it's been the constant heat and boredom. It's the stress; it's been blooming uncomfortable in that shed I can tell you.

We are definitely moving somewhere in this big noisy vehicle. It's awkward because, although we now are not so confined as in the battery cages I find myself surrounded by strangers, and we're all very fearful of strangers. I see them as a potential threat and am worried I could be attacked. They are probably equally intimidated by myself and each other. By a strange quirk of nature, we hens are incensed by the colour red, and what colour are our wattles, our eye surrounds and our combs? That's right, they're red, so we might as well sit on a bullseye and ask someone to throw darts at us.

It seems now as if some of my fellow inmates from the shed had stopped laying eggs. You see, when we get to about eighteen months old, because we haven't had a break from laying since we first began, our egg production begins to drop off, in spite of the artificial conditions. When the egg output for the whole shed falls before a certain percentage, they cull the lot of us and bring new young girls in. These youngsters are generally about eighteen weeks old, and at what is called Point of Lay. That means their egg-laying days are just beginning.

When I say cull, I really mean kill. Once we're not all laying reliably we are taken somewhere to be made into stock cubes, dog food, cheap pies, gravy granules, and so on. That could be where we're going now, although the people who lifted us out of the cages did so quite gently, they made me feel that they might care about us.

I caught sight of myself in the window of the vehicle as I was carried past. Look at me, there's not a pick of meat on me, and I've lost most of my feathers and the redness out of my comb, life in the shed has been such an ordeal. Our combs should be small and neat and stand erect, but for most of the ladies in the shed, our combs are massive and very pale, flopping over to one side very often as we try desperately to cool ourselves down. Can you imagine thousands of bodies all crammed together in a metal shed? The heat can be stifling.

Well, it's a while later and I'm still here to continue my little tale, not stock cubes or dog food at all. It had got very uncomfortable in the shed earlier, especially when the food and water supply was cut off. I suppose it saves the farmer money, and if we're about to be sent to be killed anyway there's no commercial sense in feeding us up to the last minute, however cruel that is. So, how come I'm still here? We were eventually unloaded from the big vehicle and put in a different place.

We had been quite crushed in that vehicle and I think we all thought this was the end, so we were very subdued, but when we were let out we were put in a big enclosure outside, and I mean BIG, and there was plenty of food and water and people checking us over. The area was fenced all round but out in the open, which is how hens should live. The food, and especially the water, was very welcome, and there was loads of it – as much as we wanted to drink. I think we all felt the same.

Some of the girls were so happy that they laid eggs to say thank you straight away. I can see a big sign and these people have writing on their t-shirts: *Hen Save*. Wow! They're saving us and seem to be making our lives more like real life should be. For lots of us our beaks had grown very long and the people clipped those, which was much more comfortable and made it easier for us to feed and drink. They sorted out any other health problems we had as well. Before I had time to think about all of this, we were on the move again.

Just four of us this time, and we were gently picked out and put in a cardboard box that had breathing holes in it. We had no idea what was going on. We were buffeted about a bit in what someone called a car, and there was a long queue of other cars waiting to take more of the hens from the enclosure. I thought it was a funny system if we were going to be killed, but I began to think that wasn't the plan at all. When the box was opened and we were let out, we were in another generous enclosure. It had avian mesh across the sides, which would keep us safe from foxes and stop mice from pinching our food, and it had a bit of a roof to keep the worst of the weather off. It was like heaven to see the sky and birds flying, and feel the fresh air.

Across the middle of the enclosure was a sort of lattice fence, dividing it in two. On our side of the fence were bowls of food and of water, so I had a lovely drink and some food and took a look around. We had a large, cardboard box filled with comfy-looking bedding for when we got tired. I was feeling happy enough to lay an egg now, so I got on with that and the person who'd brought us in here told me I was a clever girl. I've never heard that before; I'm a hen, it's what we do. She gave me a cuddle and a little stroke. That was a bit scary, I'd never been stroked before but it was okay, she was very gentle. Then she put a ring round my leg and told me that I had a name. My leg ring is green, and my name is Emerald.

Now I have time for a proper look around.

On the other side of the lattice fence there were four other girls looking at us intently. They were alert and interested, with red combs and eyes. I felt very ashamed of my looks with the few remaining scraggy feathers I hadn't lost through stress, and my comb pale and floppy, but they bocked away quite happily after running up and down and giving us a good look over. They had food and water of their own so there was plenty for everyone.

The other three girls I was rescued with were also given names, and the woman referred to us then as the Jewel Girls. There was Pearl with a white leg ring, Amethyst whose ring was purple, and I bet you can work out Ruby's colour for yourself.

Over the next few days we spent a short time each day with the barrier moved out of the way so we could all share the big space, until somebody got cross and then we would go back to our two separate groups. The woman stayed with us while the barrier was down, and it wasn't scary at all. If it looked like trouble was brewing she would gently move us out of the way and if that didn't diffuse the situation she would pop the barrier back up. Bit by bit we were getting used to each other. Then one morning, the other group were brought into our half one at a time, so we could meet them individually. Because they didn't have safety in numbers I suppose, they were quite submissive and gentle. As a group our person called them the Golden Girls, and their names were Rose, Blanche, Dorothy and Sophia.

After it went dark that night, we were each gently lifted out of the cardboard box where we had settled, and placed inside the proper hen coop where the Golden Girls already slept. There was a little bit of wing-flexing and feather ruffling, but we were all so tired that we soon settled down. I really feel that we have, at last, come home to roost, and it's a good feeling.

The next morning, the lattice dividing fence had gone. There were still plenty of feeders and drinkers though, and the cardboard box and a couple of obstacles we could hide behind for a while if we felt scared. There was stuff to do as well, two big old gnarled branches stretched across the open space and we watched how the Golden Girls used them to perch on. Before long we were all perching along them together. I'd never seen a perch before.

We'd sit there and have lovely chats. The Golden Girls had been with our woman when she lived at another house, and then moved here with her and her family. Rose told us that on the moving day all their big stuff was shifted in a huge van, the husband brought fragile stuff in his car and our woman dealt with the animals. The animals at that time were the Golden Girls, a couple of other hens, and a dog.

Rose said that when they arrived at the new house the next door neighbour came out to meet them and when our woman first met her she had the dog on a lead and a hen under each arm. She must have looked so funny and the new neighbour looked so surprised.

One of the other girls told me that our women found it very interesting that we are all very different temperaments. I don't know why, because she wouldn't expect all dogs or all cats to behave the same, so why should birds? She went on to tell us about a hen who lived with them at the old house. It seems that our woman had decided to add to the flock and had brought home some younger girls, just starting to lay. One sadly didn't live very long, but Violet, who was a big girl, lived to a good age. She had very dark feathers with a purple sheen. Apparently she had very fluffy feathers round her cloaca which, if you've not come across the word before, is the name for a hen's bum. She had beautiful feathery legs and it meant that from time to time she got a bit messy.

Our woman would take her indoors to her utility room, stand Violet in a couple of inches of warm water and wash her bum! I don't think many people would do that for a hen. But then it gets better. This was fine in the warm weather. Violet could go straight outside again, but when winter came our woman was worried about her catching a chill and she would gently dry her cloaca and legs with a hairdryer. They would play at being at the hairdresser, with our woman asking Violet if she was going anywhere nice for her holidays.

Violet used to tell the other girls afterwards about how she would stand with her eyes shut, thoroughly enjoying being spoiled. When the woman spread out her wings one by one to make sure she was properly dry underneath them, Violet would just leave them there when the woman let go, it felt so nice. The woman told her it was called a Pamper Day. I was astonished! You couldn't make it up.

There were lots of stories, and there was lots of food out for us too, not just the regular mash or meal in our bowls, but also fun food like lumps of cabbage, and sunflower heads or chunks of melon hanging on strings for us to peck at. Sometimes, if we pecked hard enough, we could get the hanging up food to swing and bop one of the others on the beak or on the bum, but sometimes they would get their own back by pecking it really hard, so it would come back and hit whoever had started it. We had some laughs.

I don't know who the hens were who had

dropped production to a level where the farmer decided to clear our shed, but living out here in this lovely roomy enclosure most of us are laying an egg most days. I think that's because we feel happy and safe. I try each time to lay my very best egg and the person who looks after us says they taste wonderful, nothing like shop-bought ones. It's quite different here than in that shed, much more relaxed, and nobody minds if we don't lay, we get fed and cuddled just the same. It's true, Blanche hadn't laid a single egg since we arrived, but she got treated just the same as the rest of us. It's wonderful.

The woman says we will all live out our days here, until we die of old age, and she means it. One day Blanche began to look very hunched up, which is not a good sign in hen world. She hadn't come out of the coop in the morning, until our woman came and gently lifted her out. She placed her in a corner, where she wouldn't get trodden on whilst we were running around, and she tried to tempt her with water and food, but Blanche wasn't interested and just sat there with her eyes closed.

We saw a lot of our woman that day. There's a log in one corner of the enclosure that she often sits on, and she spent a lot of time just sitting there watching over Blanche, then she'd go back into the house for a while. Eventually someone came out of the house and said: 'It's Mo Farah's second race, Mum. Come on or you're going to miss it.'

'I don't want to leave her, she's very close to the end,' she said, and there were real tears in her eyes. Then she went and got a soft, snuggly looking towel, and gently wrapped Blanche in it and took her into the house with them. We watched them go and I think we knew we'd never see Blanche alive again. We actually did see her just once more but it was when our woman brought her body out to show us. I suppose so that we weren't just left wondering.

The next day our woman was telling a neighbour that one of her hens had passed away.

'I wanted to be with her at the end,' she said, 'but I wanted to watch the race too, so I scooped her up in a towel, took her into the living room, and watched it with her on my knee. The dog came over for a quick snuffle at her, but it was as if he knew, and he went straight away to lie down. She died just after the race finished, but at least she was comfy and cuddled at the end.'

So you see, even after we stop laying I'm sure that she'll feed us and look after us as well as she can.

I'm going inside the coop to lay her an egg now. I think she deserves the best eggs we can give her in exchange for the life she's given us.

Lovely Lizzie

The first time it happened was quite unintentional. A friend had asked could she buy a copy of one of my short story volumes, *The Hairdryer died Today,* and I took it with me when we met up one day for lunch. So that it didn't get splashed with food she tucked it onto the far corner of the table. We had just started eating when a couple of smartly dressed ladies brushed past the table, but one of them stopped.

'That looks interesting. May I?'

My friend explained that I had written it and the proceeds were for charity. She immediately asked where she could get a copy. Now, it can be bought on line but if a paperback is bought directly from me, because I can buy author copies at a reduced price, then much more profit can be raised for the charity. I was starting to explain this when my friend interrupted, saying: 'Take this one. We meet up regularly and I can easily pick up another. I'm not ready to start reading it yet anyway.'

The money changed hands and I decided that in future, when I was out and about, I would carry a copy in the car with me in case this ever happened again. There are now four volumes, this one you're reading being the fourth so it's quite a haul I'm toting about. It has paid off though, most recently in a charity shop.

Going up to town is something I do quite frequently, loving to tour the charity shops in particular. Books on sale are always a favourite, but I keep an open mind. On this occasion I took a couple of paperbacks to the young lady seated behind the cash desk. She was engrossed in a book of her own.

'Sorry,' she hastily put down the book she was reading, 'I get deep in a story and lose myself.'

She started to ring up the item as I looked round the shelves, 'You're in the right place for it here, there's a great selection of books. What is it you're reading that's so engrossing?'

She handed the book across, not one I'd come across before. 'I like reading these,' she told me, 'they're quite light and short, and I'm not a very good reader. They're easy when you keep having to break off to serve people.' I wondered whether I should apologise for interrupting her, but I could see that she wasn't meaning any criticism, it was just a way of filling in the dead time for her between customers.

'Do you like reading?' she asked me, as she counted out my change.

'Yes, and writing. I work for a charity too in a small way. I write short stories to raise money for The British Deaf Association.'

'Short stories? I love reading short stories, you get such a lot of variety in one book.'

'You're right. I'm working on my fourth now, and they've each got over thirty different tales.'

'Do you never run out of ideas? Where do you get your inspiration from?'

'That's a question writers get asked a lot, and I'm afraid the answer must often disappoint, because sometimes it's impossible to know. Some of them are based on experience, mine or other people's and they may be almost entirely true, or just the bones of an idea that I adapt with made up stuff. Others I can pin down to things that people have said to me, and just got me pondering .... *I wonder* ....'

'And you never run out of things to say?' she sounded surprised.

'Not so far. I think it helps that it's for charity, people are much more likely to part with their five pounds or whatever whenever it's going to a good cause.'

Our conversation had been interrupted a couple of times by Lizzie's paying customers, and I collected my purchases and put away my purse.

'I'd like to buy one,' she said, 'it would be ideal to have something I can dip into here on the till.'

So the next time I visited town I had with me a copy of each of the first two completed volumes. The young lady, who told me her name was Lizzie, was once again on the till and recognised me.

She looked between the titles, 'I'd like that one please, I'll get you some money.' Then she spotted a colleague and called over to her, 'Anne, have you got five pounds there? I'll give it back to you when I go in the back. I've got it in my bag, but can't leave the till.'

The other lady brought a twenty pound note over, and Lizzie opened the till to get some change. It was only then that I noticed she was in a wheelchair.

I thought it was interesting that I could have two conversations with her and not notice this. She was so interesting to chat to and so vivacious, that it wasn't the first thing you noticed about her, and she clearly didn't allow it to define her. She asked for my phone number, which I was happy to provide.

A few weeks later there was a text from Lizzie. She had loved the book and would I please take her a copy of the second one when I was next in town? Of course I would. Lizzie's up to date with reading them all now, and says that she often recommends them to others in the shop. She is one of my best advocates – Lovely Lizzie.

Last Bus to Wareham

My dad sat me down in the living room, just the two of us, which in itself was weird, and said there was something we needed to discuss. This was evidently something serious, usually domestic arrangements were left up to my mother. It seemed that I had been invited on holiday to Dorset with the family of my best friend Josie. Her parents Blair and Ava thought it would be nice for their daughter to have company for the fortnight, and also for me. Theirs was a large family whereas I was an only child. They had rented two adjacent caravans on a site in Wareham, and as well as my friend Josie and her twin brothers who were eight, would be their baby sister, who was not quite old enough to walk.

I don't think I was particularly perceptive as a teenager, but Dad seemed to be trying to get across some message that was more than just the words he was saying. Things like 'You can phone home if you need us; we can come and get you if you're very unhappy. It's only a couple of hours' drive away.' I could think of no reason why he might be saying things like that. Why would I be unhappy on a holiday with my best friend? My dad was an abstemious man, and I had no idea then that my friend's father Blair, whom I had only met a few times, was subject to bouts of drunkenness and rage, often resulting in violence against his timid wife, and possibly against his children too. He was a well-known and well-respected businessman. If I said his name you would be aware of his companies.

It was, I think, three evenings into the holiday that I noticed a shift in demeanour among my host family. Josie and I had been allocated one caravan along with the suitcases and other paraphernalia that accompanies a large family on holiday, whereas the parents, the boys and the baby slept in the other. I never even entered that caravan during the whole of the fortnight.

There was only one television and that was in 'our' van, the van we all used during the days, for meals, and spending time together. I had not seen a great deal of Blair. He was, so his wife told me as we washed the dishes, not interested in television, and preferred to read quietly in other van in the evenings. I accepted this at face value, why wouldn't I? My parents were both keen readers, who would often spend the evenings with their books rather than the television, and what reason would there possibly be to lie?

It was not until quite late that evening, after the baby had been put to bed, that we heard a car screech to a halt outside the van. Ava immediately told the boys to go into the other van and change for bed, and it was only then that I realised that Blair had been out on his own for several hours. She turned the volume on the television right down, so that we could hardly hear it, and Josie and her mother sat nervously watching the caravan door.

Blair burst in red-faced and belligerent, taunting all of us to rise to what he was saying. I started to argue but Josie's mother silently shook her head, and I began to see that this must be what my father had been warning me about. My friend lived a life of being bullied, and watching her mother and brothers suffer the same fate. It was something beyond my understanding. When we were alone Josie felt the need to explain. Her father was perfectly fine most of the time, but became aggressive when drunk, which was not a frequent occurrence, but often enough. She suspected that the baby, lovely as she was, was probably the product of his rape of her mother. I foolishly asked how she could stand it, and she looked at me as if it was a ridiculous question, which I suppose it was. She asked what choice she had – none. She would stay as long as she had to, then leave home once the boys were old enough to keep an eye on their mum and the baby.

This explained my dad's tête-à-tête. He must have been aware, or at least suspicious, of Blair's tendencies. I vowed to myself never to get on the wrong side of Blair's temper and I managed it too, until the very last evening of the holiday.

Josie and I had been given permission to go into Swanage by ourselves on the bus. It took a quaint route, winding up and down the hills from village to village, sometimes waiting for regulars who weren't yet at the bus stop. At one point the driver turned off the engine and went to knock on a front door, then waited back in his seat for that passenger to join us.

He didn't comment on it, neither did the individual involved. I wondered if it was a routine part of the journey.

By the time we pulled into Swanage for our exciting evening out, feeling very grown up, it was twenty to nine. We had been given strict instructions to get the last bus back and make sure we didn't miss it. As we left the bus, I asked the driver what time the last bus for Wareham left Swanage. He looked at his watch, and said: 'This is it, love. We leave in twelve minutes.'

Twelve minutes! Twelve minutes to paint the town red? There wasn't even time to find a café never mind go in and order a coke. A coke we wouldn't have time to drink. Instead we stood in the bus shelter, scrabbling through our purses and bags to see how much change we had; would we be able to afford a taxi? We decided that we would, and went off in search of the coke.

As evenings go it wasn't a great success, but we felt very grown up sitting in a milk bar, chatting to a couple of other girls. Just before ten we decided that we should find a taxi, and get back to the caravan site. We agreed that there was no need to mention the taxi; if asked about the bus journey we could just talk about the outward bound journey and nobody would be any the wiser. Except . . .

Except that the taxi driver pulled up at the gate to the caravan site to drop us off, as we had asked and we sat counting out our change. We didn't have quite enough to cover the fare! Josie was clearly concerned that we might have to go and ask her parents to make up the difference, but he waived it, saying nice things like, 'It was a joy having two such lovely girls in his cab.' This he repeated through the open window as he drove away.

Unfortunately, as you've no doubt guessed, Blair had gone to the pub while we were out and arrived back at the entrance to the caravan site just as the taxi driver was shouting about what lovely girls we were. He didn't even slow the car or glance our way as he drove past us, and was sitting in the caravan waiting for us by the time we had walked there from the gate.

If the ensuing scene had happened any earlier in the holiday; if we hadn't in any case been going home the next day, then I may have been doing as my dad suggested and phoning home for someone to come and get me. How do families live like this? The abuse was awful, language such as I had never heard, suggesting that the taxi driver may have been offered favours in return for the journey, even after we showed Blair our empty purses. Totally dismissed was the idea that it was unreasonable to go for an evening out and return after twelve minutes. The haranguing went on and on. I could only follow Josie's lead as she sat silently obedient and took it all. Her mother hovered by and I reflected later that our behaviour that evening had probably made life more difficult for her, which was a shame. Eventually Blair stormed out, and Ava just shook her heads at us. The expression that popped into my head was, *'more in sorry than in anger,'* before she followed him across to the other caravan.

It was only a matter of months before Josie and her family moved away. Blair had received a better job offer, and although Josie and I kept up a desultory correspondence for a while, the closeness had gone.

It was over twenty years later when, purely by chance, my job brought me into contact once again with Josie. Blair had not enjoyed his new job and after a couple of years he had left to become the landlord of a small, rural pub in a remote area of Shropshire, not at all well served by buses as she told me. She herself had not spoken to Blair for over a decade. He had not attended her wedding, nor had he met her children, but she was close to her mother and siblings. I felt sorry for Ava, who seemed to be in the middle of this rift, trying to pacify everybody. According to what she had told Josie, Blair was much happier in the pub, more amenable and I think that made sense. He could hardly make a scene of the kind I had witnessed in a pub that provided his livelihood and that of his family. He could, I suppose drink copiously and then go upstairs to bed, not having to drive home. Perhaps it was ideal for him.

My path and Josie's passed tangentially another fifteen years later, in that a colleague of my sister's used to frequent the pub where Blair was landlord. By then Blair was long dead and Ava had remarried, a gentle and calm man, who treated her well. I was relieved. She had suffered a hard life and deserved some good fortune.

The Fungarium

He wasn't a particularly resourceful man, nor a man at one with nature, but Arthur was blessed with a large garden, and he wanted to maximise its use. He enjoyed growing things, particularly chrysanthemums, which he nurtured carefully and entered into the county show each year.

Each year that is, until his young grandson *helped* in Arthur's greenhouse when nobody was looking, by gathering up all the nametags he could reach out of each plant pot. He was busy playing with them on the path when Arthur went back into the garden after a restorative cup of tea. The name labels were all mixed up, and he had no way of knowing which variety was which; which should be left to their own devices, which should be stopped; which lightly pruned, which disbudded, which were ready for pollinating and so on.

The child was too young to know any better and Arthur blamed himself, but it would be pure guesswork whether any of his blooms were fit to be shown at this year's show, and he decided to have a year off. He had four beehives down on a rough patch at the bottom of the garden, but these nowhere near filled his time, so he was casting around for a new interest.

Mushrooms! He read an article about their cultivation in the *Amateur Gardening* magazine and decided to have a go. A container of mushroom spores was duly bought and delivered, much to his excitement. The magazine article had suggested that these would grow well in the dark. The cellar was declared by Arthur to be ideal, and he spent most of one day spreading soil and the mushroom spores across the dark, damp soil floor. Then he waited.

And waited. And waited. And waited some more. Nothing happened. No mushrooms, not a single one, and it was almost time to start working on selection, sowing and potting up of next year's chrysanthemums. Disappointed, he shovelled up the soil and spore mixture from the cellar floor, carrying bucketful after bucketful upstairs, outside and spreading them as a fertilizer across the back garden flower beds.

Three weeks later he opened the curtains one morning to a bizarre sight. Overnight it seemed that all the mushrooms had thrust through the loamy soil. Burgeoning between all his ornamental flowers and vegetables was a sea of small, white domes. These days mycologists know that the growth of mushrooms is not dependent on light levels and that they will grow equally happily in light or in the dark; it is usually just recommended to grow them in the dark as it is cheaper, no electricity being needed.

Arthur wrote a letter to his magazine asking for their opinion, and he was told that almost certainly it was the disturbance of the loam from the cold cellar floor into the comparatively warm spring soil outdoors that had triggered growth. They apologised that he had not been satisfied with his purchase, although his letter was more driven by curiosity than complaint, and they offered another free shipment of mushroom spores.

Arthur thought for a while. The house seemed to be coming down with mushrooms, they were everywhere and the family and neighbours were sick of being given presents of them. He refused the magazine's offer. He would enjoy what he had, then go back to his beloved chrysanthemums. As long as you keep the identifying markers out of the way of little fingers, you know where you are with chrysanthemums.

The Prophet of Doom

Marilyn and Aiden had been married for six years and lived in a flat in London. She was fortunate in that Aiden earned sufficient for them to be comfortable; not extravagant, but comfortable and she could pick and choose which part time jobs she fancied. Except when Aiden was hit with a deep depression, which had happened a couple of times, but they had always managed to weather the storm. To Marilyn's mind a bit of a challenge now and then made their bond stronger. She would have liked to have children, but none had come along and Aiden had never seemed bothered, so they were quite an insular unit.

New Year's Eve could sometimes be a bit of a downer, Marilyn understood that, but towards the end of 2014 Aiden had seemed to be getting more and more despondent. In fact, thinking back, she had been worried about his mental health for a while. It seemed that for the past couple of years he had been very bothered about his job, about politics here at home and on the world stage. He would not consider getting help or taking medication, he felt it more manly to soldier on.

The two of them didn't make a big fuss about Christmas. They mainly set aside a sum of money and each went clothes shopping, then they each had a small present to open on Christmas morning.

This year Marilyn had been particularly happy with her choice. Aiden had always been interested in history. He sometimes said he wished he'd studied it more when he was younger, and she had found a Historical facts book that had kept him entranced throughout the whole of Christmas Day.

It was as early as Boxing Day that he said something mildly concerning. With one finger in the book marking his page, he came to breakfast and plonked himself down in front of his usual bowl of cereal.

'I never realised,' he said, 'that so many significant events happened in years ending in five.'

'Really?' Marilyn vaguely wondered whether they had enough milk to last until Monday or whether she should go out. Would the village shop even be open? She hadn't checked. 'Like what?'

'Where to begin,' he said, 'It would take too long to go through them all, but most of them are pretty bad.' He then seemed to have a good go at going through them all. He must have had this list committed to memory,

'Magna Carta 1215, The Wars of the Roses started 1455, the Gunpowder Plot 1605, The Great Plague 1665, Battle of Trafalgar 1805, Battle of Waterloo 1815, Hiroshima 1945.'

'But they aren't all bad are they?' Marilyn tried to lighten the tone. 'We were successful at Trafalgar and Waterloo. Hiroshima helped bring about the end of World War II. You have to look on the bright side, Aiden.' She began to wonder whether the book had been such a good idea. Her husband had a tendency to get despondent about things quite irrationally.

Not deigning to reply, he spent most of the day and evening poring over the book, making copious notes and timelines. Eventually, as they prepared for bed that night he said: '2015 in a couple of days, something bad is destined to happen. The signs are all there, look.'

Marilyn sighed quietly and turned her back on him, 'I'm tired now, love. Can I look tomorrow?'

'It won't go away whatever it is Marilyn, just because you turn your back on it. It'll still be there tomorrow.'

'So we'll talk about it then, eh?' she said sleepily.

The following morning Aiden went back to work, and Marilyn set about cleaning the flat. In the spare bedroom, which Aiden had commandeered as his study, she came across the lists and charts that he had drawn, and was amazed at the trouble he had taken. He had interspersed detailed notes with sketches – coffins against his notes about 1665, a battlefield by the eighteen hundreds, and the iconic image of a mushroom cloud against the atomic bomb narrative of the twentieth century. It seemed that he had not found anything positive to note down.

After work Aiden was late home, and came back to the flat laden with history books from the library. Determined to help him Marilyn had spent some time leafing through the book she had given to him, and had some notes to show him when they had eaten.

'See Aiden, good things happened in years ending in five as well; in 1835 Christmas Day became a national holiday.'

'Tell that to the people who work in retail,' he muttered, and she had to concede that he had a fair point.

'Okay, in 1855 the first pillar box was erected in London.' She waited for the rebuttal but not came, 'and in 1865 Joseph Lister first used carbolic acid on a patient to disinfect a wound.'

'I bet that stung,' was all he said, before taking himself off to the study, and back to the books and his lists.

After another few evenings watching him mope about she resolved to put the book in the bin. It wasn't doing his mental health any good to be so maudlin, and it was making her twitchy. She took the books back to the library too, and brought home instead a couple of lighthearted paperbacks.

On New Year's Eve he came home from work and went straight to the study, emerging almost immediately, 'Where's my stuff?'

'I threw it away and took the library books back, I'll get you something else as a belated Christmas present. This obsession isn't healthy.'

'I don't want something else. That was a book you gave to me, you had no right to throw it away. It's not an obsession, it's my research.'

'I'm sorry, Aiden, it seems to be making you so depressed. We'll get you something more cheerful in the sales. Come on and get changed, we're at the party next door tonight. Don't forget, it's New Year's Eve.'

'I'm not going,' he remained stubbornly at the table, 'You go. I'm just being miserable. You'll have more fun without me anyway. I'll be fine.' He managed a smile. 'Go on, enjoy yourself.'

When she got home just after midnight Aiden had gone to bed and was snoring gently. In the study the book, his notes and charts had been retrieved from the bin, wiped clean and replaced on the table. Marilyn sighed quietly and turned off the light.

The following morning he seemed more cheerful, perhaps he had taken her words to heart.

'I'm okay love, I really am. I just find all this stuff interesting that's all. And you're quite right, good things happen in years ending in five as well as bad. And other years have bad things happen. It's not the number five that's having a bad impact.'

For the next two weeks life drifted along as normal. Aiden seemed to be back to his old self, and Marilyn began to breathe more easily.

Then on the fifteenth, the day the press had begun to call 'Black Monday' as being the most depressing of the year, he was home early from work, and was sitting at the desk in the study when she arrived back from the shops.

'I knew it,' he turned on her, 'I warned you, and nobody would listen. I'd been phoning them all at work telling them 2015 was going to be a bad year, and you all pooh-poohed it as nonsense. Well, I was right. And I was proved right today, the fifteenth.'

'Right? How were you proved right? What's happened?'

'The company's gone into liquidation that's what happened! We all got there this morning to find the door locked and the shutters down. We've no money coming in now, I'm fifty-five, I'll never get another job at my age. I warned you,' a touch of hysteria hit his voice, 'I warned the whole lot of you!

'Happy New Year, Marilyn! Happy sodding New Year!'

Splash

It was late December. The weather was dreadful, gale force winds and driving rain but Mikey was very firmly of the opinion that he would never be just a fair-weather dog walker. Dogs need and want exercise regardless of the weather.

So the heaviest waterproof winter coat and boots were added to woolly hat and gloves and the expedition set off. The dog was soaked, but joyously snuffling at all the new smells laid down overnight, until at last they turned off the by-ways and approached the kerb to cross the main road.

It was quite deliberate. A large battered white van scribed with red lettering, swerved towards the footpath for no reason other than to drive through an enormous puddle in the gutter, soaking both man and dog. The face of the young man driving broke into a huge grin, as he made rude gestures out of the window. Not quick enough to note the number, nevertheless, as the vehicle made a right turn into a side road, Mikey noticed that previous damage to the vehicle had left just half a logo on the driver's side, where the door had evidently been replaced but not painted to match.

It took a further twenty minutes for Mikey and the dog to reach home. The waterproof coat was soaked from the rain anyway as well as the splash from the puddle bow-wave; his boots seemed to be full of water and his jeans were wet up to the crotch. The wet clothes were easily dealt with and the dog soon dried after a much-needed shower.

Mikey was not a vengeful person, and the incident was all but forgotten by the following July. Then he recognised the same van. It had a logo on the sides and the back doors, but the damaged door had not been repainted and the driver's door was plain white. It was definitely the same one, and when he looked up there was the same young man.

The van was parked in a private driveway on Back Lane, a pretty little lane with properties only on one side. They were slightly elevated from the road, which gave them a lovely view of the fields and open land opposite. The van was nose-in to the property and both back doors were wide open. Back Lane was narrow, with a strip of grass along the built-up side, but drivers needed to be careful as they passed, there being so little room. Approaching the drive where the van was parked, Mikey was forced to slow down, as a car was approaching him, travelling too fast in his opinion. With the fields to his left, he swerved over as close to the hedge as he could, slowed right down and watched the drama unfold.

As the car approached the drive where the van was parked, Mikey could see that a hosepipe was stretched out down the path beside the van, and the same young man who had splashed him months earlier was walking up the slope of what was, presumably, his own driveway. The hosepipe was still spurting water, and Mikey assumed that the man was going to turn off a tap somewhere on the building, having finished washing the van.

Mikey's assailant had just reached the front of his vehicle when the car coming the other way took evasive action to avoid hitting the front of Mikey's car. The driver swerved sharply to his left, hitting a puddle created by the still-flowing water from the hosepipe. As there was not a conventional footpath, but just the grass verge, the water in the gutter was very muddy. Mikey sat and watched mesmerised as a bow-wave, not unlike the one he had been treated to the previous December, arced up from the road, soaking the newly-cleaned van with muddy water. As the back doors were fully open, the inside of the van too was treated to a mud bath.

Mikey liked to think that he was not unkind, and he would certainly never had sought out the young man to take any sort of pleasure in his misfortunate. However it did give him cause to smile as he looked in his mirror and saw the man, who had now walked back down his drive and was standing with his hands on his hips looking in bemusement at the devastation around his newly-cleaned van.

Mikey found himself whistling a cheerful little tune all the way home, and for some reason he could not define, the dog was given a larger-than-usual dinner that night.

Scooters for All

Were we particularly naïve in the nineteen fifties and early sixties? Or perhaps unworldly is a better word. As children we had fewer expectations and were more easily satisfied. We never expected to be driven to school; whatever the weather we knew that we would be walking, sometimes with our mother, grandmother or aunt. Then when we were a little older, we walked in the charge of our older cousin. She was four years my senior and would always walk ahead of us as if she didn't know us at all. The only time her responsibility came to the fore that I can remember is when I was skipping with a rope. The rope was meant to have been left at home, but it was new and had ball bearings in the handles, which gave it a very smooth action and I didn't want to be parted from it, even just for the length of the school day.

Unfortunately my action in skipping with it was not so smooth, and skipping along on the way to school I missed my footing and landed on my knees. Helen picked me up and spat on her hanky before wiping my knees, and my tears. She rolled the rope up and put it in her own schoolbag, then walked me in to the school office, where she said that I had fallen over. They patched me up, and my mother never found out about the illicit rope.

But this story is about scooters. Not these e-scooters that one sees nowadays. I am talking about a very simple construction, little handlebars on a height-adjustable handle, a narrow footplate and two wheels. No brakes, you put your foot on the floor to stop it.

I don't remember his scooter being given to my oldest cousin Jonathan, who was Helen's big brother. It was his Christmas present a year or so before I was born. He was eight years older than I, but I remember he played with it a lot while I was a toddler and a small child, I recall that distinctly. It was blue with yellow centres to the wheels, and a triangular maker's name on the handlebars.

As he outgrew the scooter Helen played on it more and more. Then, one Christmas I remember she was given a scooter of her own, a shiny pink and white one with silver and pink stickers. It had little coloured streamers, again pink and silver hanging from each of the handlebars. I remember her standing me on the footplate and putting my little hands onto the handlebars, then she would scoot along the garden path we me shrieking with laughter in front of her as the streamers moved about and tickled my hands.

Occasionally, when Helen wasn't around, I was allowed to play with the scooter by myself but she was very proprietorial about it. At this time too, with Jonathan at senior school, Helen in Junior school and myself in the Infants' we saw less of them. There was homework and hobby clubs for the older ones outside of school hours, and eventually Helen's scooter was relegated to the shed where it was forgotten. I never knew what happened to it, but on my birthday I was given a new scooter of my own, a deep blue one. I asked Helen if we could ride them together but she said that she was going out with her friends. I played by myself, but I did pass on the privilege of riding a scooter to my younger brother, Matt, in the way Helen had done for me, standing him on the footplate and scooting him along. He enjoyed it I think almost as much as I had done.

The Christmas that I was six I was given a bike for my birthday, two wheels, chrome everywhere, and very much my pride and joy. My young brother was given a scooter of his own, bright purple with silver-painted wheels. He loved to play on it, although on my bike I always won our races.

A fortnight ago, and I'm twenty five now, I was sorting out the shed for my mother and I found Matt's purple scooter. I went inside the house to ask my mother what she wanted me to do with it.

'Matt's scooter?' she laughed, 'You mean the one and only scooter that any of you four ever had? The scooter that was painted and tarted up so the next owner wouldn't recognise it? I suppose if it's anybody's that it should belong to Jonathan.'

I gaped at her. I had genuinely no idea. Twenty five years old and I had never twigged, and I don't think any of the others had either, that it was the same scooter lovingly painted and polished, and handed down through the family.

Don't Mess with the Bride

Everything my future mother-in-law, Mollie, stood for rubbed me up the wrong way from the first moment I met her. I had been married and divorced, and she had apparently been very fond of my future husband's previous girlfriend, and was devastated when she had called off the plans for their marriage, so it seems that our antipathy was mutual right from the start. I can understand that she may have been concerned for her son, but honestly, he's an adult quite able to make his own decisions. She really got my back up when I overheard her referring to me as a *scarlet woman* to one of her friends. So we were never destined to be best buddies.

We went round to announce that we were to be married, (we had never officially been engaged) and told her and my future father-in-law to keep the date free. She was clearly taken aback. She eyed up my purple streaked hair, my tattoos, my Doc Martens and ripped jeans, and sighed deeply.

I knew that they were very religious people, Roman Catholics I think, and that their beloved daughter and her husband had toed the conventional line, marrying with a full mass, and popping out children at regular intervals.

That was not the life for us. My partner and I discussed what compromises we were prepared to make about our wedding day to keep his family, particularly his mother, on board, but we were united in shying away from the conventional. It was a bit alarming therefore to answer the doorbell on the morning following our announcement, to find a shy-looking priest standing there awkwardly. He told me that Mollie had contacted him, asked him to call round to discuss our plans for the service and to confirm the booking at his church.

A much more pleasant and intuitive person than Mollie, he had guessed that his visit would be unwelcome, but he seemed a lovely chap and we invited him in for a cup of coffee. We talked for quite a while, not about how we could get one over on her exactly, although I confess that this was my motive in part. At the end of our discussion we had agreed that he need not 'report back' to Mollie, as I would contact her and discuss our wedding ceremony with her, which I did. I phoned her and told her that he and I had made our plans and what a lovely man he was. I swear I could feel her preening over the phone.

That was one problem sorted or at least deferred. She need not know yet that the booking we had agreed was at the Register Office in the Town Hall, and not at his church. Now I moved onto the one concession my partner and I had agreed on: my dress for the occasion.

I really did not want the meringue-like, frilly conventional sort of affair that my partner's sister had worn, but I agreed with Mollie and my future sister-in-law that the three of us would go dress shopping together. My own mother and sister are very laid back, probably where I get it from, and were quite okay with my plans. I eventually selected the simplest, least ostentatious dress that I could find. Mollie was keen that the dress should cover my sleeve tattoos and I even gave in to that. It was only going to be for a couple of hours; on one day. My future husband and I would then have the rest of our lives together to live exactly as we pleased.

A phone call from the dress shop a couple of days later changed my mind. The manager felt that as the bride I was entitled to know that Mollie and my future sister-in-law had been back to the shop and ordered and paid for, in their own respective sizes, identical dresses to the one I had agreed to. They had unilaterally decided to wear the same white wedding dresses. They were planning to upstage me at my own wedding!

Who would do that to their son and their brother? I was outraged, as was my partner. I was very grateful to the woman in the shop and told her I would call in later in the week. Having talked it over with my partner, we agreed a plan of action. I spoke to my own mother and my sister and had their full support. The three of us went to the shop, cancelled my original order and instead ordered for the three of us, beautiful dresses in a deep bottle green.

It was my favourite colour, but one that Mollie would definitely have felt inappropriate for a wedding. She would have disapproved of green even for a guest as being unlucky, never mind for the bride. Also, the dresses were sleeveless so the tattoos she so detested would be on full view and on all the photographs. The shop manager was very apologetic about breaking Mollie's confidence, but felt, quite rightly, that she shouldn't be allowed to spoil my day. I reassured her that I was very grateful and she promised to say nothing about the changes to my order when their two dresses were collected.

It was time to send out the invitations. To my future in-laws we wrote a personal note saying that the dress code was whatever they felt comfortable in. I suspect that the disappointment at the event being held at the Register Office would be overshadowed by the thought that she had got one over on us. I could imagine her and her daughter cackling about it like a couple of witches.

To all the other female guests we suggested that if any of them were married and still had their wedding dresses it would be fun to give them another airing. For everybody else I suggested that the ladies should wear white or as light a colour as possible. Many of our friends had married in the previous couple of years and commended us on a lovely idea that made them too feel special on our wedding day.

It worked so well on the day that I was euphoric. We had arranged for a car to collect my future in-laws and take them to the service. Mollie and my new sister-in-law didn't stand out as anybody of note at the ceremony. They were just one of a crowd of guests wearing white, many of them also wearing white wedding dresses, and the two of them certainly weren't anything special. My mother and sister on the other hand, complementing my green dress as they did, looked like we three were the stars of the show. I think Mollie was still in shock from us having sent a car to take them to the ceremony. They must have worked out the reason when they were driven, not to the church, but to the Town Hall.

Mollie's sour look of disgust mellowed slightly when she saw her parish priest making his way to the front of the town hall's function room where the ceremony was being held. She truly believed that we were having a religious ceremony of some sort, in spite of being very clearly told that we weren't. The smile faded a little when the priest took up the microphone and introduced the officiating Registrar, and then went on to tell everybody that he himself had been given the great honour of performing as Master of Ceremonies at the disco, which would be held after the ceremony. He was a massive fan of heavy metal music and told us all that he had spent some happy hours choosing a wonderful selection to play for us.

It was worth it all to see Mollie's face; our wedding photographs were beautiful, our green dresses received nothing but compliments, and she and her daughter have never again tried to get one over on me.

The Junk Drawer

'Why do we keep a drawer full of clutter?' Isla had asked the question of her son, Fergus before he went out. She was trying to open the drawer and, as usual, it had jammed.

'It may come in useful one day, I suppose,' he shrugged as he left.

'I'm sorting it today,' she said to the empty room, 'I'm sure half of this stuff can be thrown away, and we won't even notice. I expect everyone has a drawer like this, which just gets more and more full until it won't close anymore. Or, if it closes, then it won't open, there is so much stuff crammed in it.' Another hefty tug and the drawer surrendered. She made herself a cup of tea, and emptied some of the contents of the drawer onto the kitchen table. So much of this stuff could surely be thrown away.

A part-filled book of Green Shield Stamps,
Two button batteries – kept just in case,
Long dried-up biros,
Broken pencils; (no sharpener),

Perished rubber bands probably dropped by the postman,
A tarnished Boy Scout badge,
Sanitised hand wipes there since the pandemic and maybe dried out now,
Three Christmas cracker gifts – nail clippers, a mini screwdriver and a tape measure,
A man's broken watch.

A man's broken watch. She remembered so well when her husband had been given it. It was when their daughter received her first proper month's salary. She said her father had helped her so much while she was studying at school, and more recently supporting her through college. He had deserved a present. She bought the watch at a specialist retailer in the city. It was beautiful, with a large, clear face. Very traditional and not very practical, and now it was broken. Isla had thought Fergus might one day wear it but he had laughed at the idea. With a phone in his hand all the time, and much more sophisticated Fitbits and so on, there had seemed no point in getting it repaired for him. And yet it held special memories. She sighed. What else was there?

The price list for the local takeaway,
The triangular key with no name that allows access to the meter cupboards,
SCART leads and cables; an old birthday candle,
Fuses, six paper napkins, and a sieve with no handle,
Last year's poppy,
An almost-dried up marker pen,
A bulldog clip, and a long-expired voucher for soap,
First class stamps; but of the old style. Were they even

legal now?
Then she came upon a tiny unopened cellophane packet.

A tiny unopened packet containing one spare button from a long-forgotten garment, along with a twist of the right coloured threads; and then she remembered. It was from Mother's bed jacket, bought for her from an upmarket shop when her final illness was first diagnosed. The jacket had been worn and worn, routinely washed and dried within the same day because Mother found it comfortable and cosy, almost like a comfort blanket. Perhaps because her daughter bought it; perhaps because it was her favourite colour combination, a subtle blend of turquoise and lilac, soft and restful. After she passed away nobody felt comfortable keeping the bed jacket, lovely though it was, and it was packed away along with other clothes and belongings and sent to the charity shop. There was something nostalgic about the button. Isla sighed. She turned her attention back to the drawer's contents.

Rawl plugs, different sizes and one of them used,
Three old pound coins from before the shape changed,
A walnut she had used for removing scratches off a wooden cupboard,
An Allen key,
A Christmas tree decoration that was only found on the floor after the box had been put into the loft,
A plastic toy soldier who wouldn't stand upright,
Having been ravaged by the dog,
A couple of toothpicks,
A part-used packet of lettuce seeds,
A locket with no hinge.

A locket with no hinge; the parting gift from Isla's first boss when she worked on Saturdays in a jewellery shop. Whilst she was still on probation the boss had watched her serve one of her first customers.

She could see at once that this couple was a cut above the shop's usual clientele. She made a point of calling over the boss, who was hovering, watching how she managed to make a sale. 'Madam, I'll just get Mr L, the owner of the business to come and serve you. I feel you really need to take advantage of his vast experience and skill.' Isla really milked it; her boss was delighted and made a great sale. This couple had never been in the shop before, but became regular customers, spending a great deal, and each year for the three years as Isla worked her way through college, she received a Hanukkah card from them.

When she left to take up a full time job, she and her fiancé having bought her engagement ring from Mr L, he presented Isla with the locket as a parting gift, saying she was the best Saturday girl he ever had. That held so many memories, it would be going back in the drawer. She was not finished yet.

A tin-plate canary that no longer sings, its key having been misplaced,
A plectrum for the guitar nobody plays,
Cotton buds, covered in pet hair,
A sachet of tomato ketchup and one of sugar - stolen from a motorway service station on their last holiday together,
An old plastic water pistol that no longer works, but whose aim is enough to stop the dog from barking,
Last year's diary,

A box with two sticking plasters – one enormous and one tiny – both pretty useless,
Various emery boards,
Two post-it notes each with a telephone number she didn't recognise,
A dog tag.

A dog tag. Not a military one, but from a real dog. Not her current dog, but from Scamp, who had sadly succumbed to cancer a couple of years before. It was rather worn around the hole where it attached to the dog's collar. They had never, for any of their dogs, added the dog's own name to their tags, so strangers could not use it to call the dog. She'd kept it, in case their current dog's tag should ever have a problem. There was some wear value still in it, in an emergency so that their dog was legal. But it would always be Scamp's tag. Scamp, the dog who had made them say, 'Never again. We can't go through the pain of losing another dog like this.' But also whose death led to the empty house when they came home, no greeting, no silly excitement, until they found themselves once again viewing the beauties that the rehoming shelter had on offer, and Lily became their new special friend. What else?

A bottle opener,
A Lego policeman,
A clutch of safety pins, all fastened together,
Spare bulbs for Christmas tree lights, whether for the current set or a previous one she wasn't sure,
A sticky tape dispenser, useful except she hadn't a roll of tape to fit it,
A tube of lip salve – maybe still viable,

> *Phillips head screws, two of them brass,*
> *A pickle fork,*
> *A bookmark her daughter had worked in cross stitch.*
> *She reached to the back of the drawer. Something was stuck. It was a photograph.*

It was a photograph. The corner had folded back and become wedged. The subject was Fergus, with very, very short hair. She smiled at it. He must have been fifteen. It was taken in their favourite holiday retreat in the Canary Islands and must have been October half term. She remembered that much earlier in the year – Easter perhaps – he said that he wanted to cut his hair. A crew cut or skinhead they called it when she was young. It was again fashionable. School had given an edict that if boys were following this current fashion, the clipper blades must be set at number 2, anything shorter was unacceptable.

Isla had suggested that, if he was going to do this, he did it at the start of the six-week' summer holiday. If he didn't like it, it would have time to grow out a bit before the new school year started. Instead he waited until she was away for the weekend at a wedding, just before school resumed, and the first she knew of it was a text from his older sister, 'Everything's fine here, Mum. Fergus's hair doesn't look TOO bad.'

She remembered the feeling of dread as they drove home, but the reality was much better than her imaginings. His hair quite suited him, and at least it was neat and consistently clipped. There was no adverse comment from school either, but looking at this photo now, taken so many weeks later, it must have been incredibly short at the time. She kissed the photo and smoothed the creased corner between finger and thumb. There were just a few more items now:

Her daughter's snuggle, made up of part of one of her original Bunnykins flannelette cot sheets, cut down and washed again and again, but this one remaining piece was one that Isla couldn't bear to part with. She put it up to her face, but there was no longer any scent,
A letter opener, seldom used with a mother of pearl handle,
And what was this? Wedged at the back?
A torch!

A torch! Isla took it out and unscrewed the base. There were no batteries in it now, but the compartment was rusted and dry. It took her right back to her daughter, at eight years old. Never a good sleeper, the little girl would read well into the night, by the light of this torch, a birthday present she had loved. She would hide under the bedclothes with the torch, perhaps for fear of being stopped, or probably just because it was an adventure.

That was the year her interest in books first began. Her favourite; another birthday present, was The Clockmender's Shop, a picture book illustrated with all different styles of brightly-coloured clocks, each with its own story.

The torch had four different colour settings, produced by means of a multi-coloured disc. She read with it almost every night and never seemed to realise, or certainly never commented, that the batteries didn't run down. Night after night the little girl would eventually fall asleep over her book. Isla would tuck her in before going to bed herself, turn off the torch, and tuck it and the book underneath her pillow. Periodically she would replace the batteries, but her daughter never seemed to notice.

Now she looked at all these things spread on the table, all these memories, and Isla knew that she couldn't part with most of this stuff, clutter or not. This drawer was a repository that held so many memories. Clearing it would require some decisions she didn't want to make. Not now, not today. With one quick movement of her arm it was all swept back into the drawer.

The Pan Gremlins

My, my, my! It seems that a Gremlin's work is never done. I'm exhausted.

Hi, I'm Pan, short for Pandora. One of many Pans actually, there is a massive team of us working nationwide. You probably won't have heard of us and you certainly won't have seen us, but I can absolutely guarantee that if you have travelled in a vehicle recently you will be familiar with our many achievements, and we seem to become busier and busier all the time. For we are the Pan Pothole Gremlins, and our job is constructing, maintaining and developing all the potholes in the country's roads. We make up a massive team and we're kept very busy.

There haven't always been Pothole Gremlins, because there haven't always been roads and there haven't always been potholes. It was one woman; one careless woman called Pandora, who broke the family's cooking pot and started it all many years ago. I believe that our story has often been told in the years since, but, not believing the reality, people wrote about her having a box containing all sorts of awful things and emotions. The reality is that the original

Pandora went down to the edge of the track outside her hut and dug out enough clay to make a replacement pot to cook the family's evening meal. She baked it all day over the open fire to waterproof it, and it was as simple as that. It worked well, the clay held all the liquids in the meal without leaking, and she popped the pot away in the corner of her hut for future use.

What she didn't know was that not only clay was released from the hole she had dug that day. It was a deep hole, the bottom of which broke through the roof of our kingdom, releasing a colony of Pothole Gremlins onto the world, all of us called Pandora, Pan for short.

At that time there was less concern about holes in the roads. The wheel had been, long before, a great move forward for people and there had been little improvement in road building since. People coped with the expected failures and broken axles and whatnot, deeming it small price to pay to be able to move about.

Nowadays it's very different. People feel that they are entitled to travel about unencumbered by our handiwork and we're not appreciated at all.

Like everybody we have friends and we have those we really can't get on with. One particular ally is the weather, especially rain when followed by ice or a crisp, sharp frost. The water that falls as rain spreads to fill a hole, pushing at the corners where it has gathered, doing our work for us. Another help is tree roots that damage the surface of paths, and sometimes roads, especially now that it is more than a hundred years since the start of the Victorian era, when so many were planted. The roots on those mature trees often struggle to continue growing downwards and so shift the tarmac or asphalt across the surface. In doing so, they help us immensely.

I told you about rain being our particular friend, well we also have two particular enemies who work cleverly in conjunction with each other to try and defeat us. One is the Highways Agency whose work in monitoring and filling in potholes is nearly as diligent as our own. Our other enemy is money; money in the hands of the necessary authorities to be able to buy the equipment and filler to deal with our handiwork. Fortunately for us, money is currently in short supply and the only remedial action that can be taken for a lot of the holes is patching.

In our regular team meetings we often talk about patching. It is the biggest waste of money that the authorities could possibly carry out, which delights us. They fill in a pothole with a patch, invariably of a different medium from the surrounding surface, so it often doesn't bond properly. So then the sun, wind, rain, frost – whatever, work their magic as well as traffic running over it, and before we know it, we're well on the way to another pothole. I do feel a bit sorry for the workers sometimes. It must be a thankless task, and they must know that at the best it's a temporary fix, even without our interference. It works well for us of course. We are targeted with keeping the holes open, and adding to them, so there's no way we're going to teach them their job.

I've told you how busy we are, but we have to stop now and then to take on our version of food, to keep us going. Food for us is asphalt, tarmacadam, even concrete or rubble. It's helpful that, while we are going around doing our job we can nibble off bits of pot holes as we go, as well as helping their progress along.

People have cameras on their phones these days. They take their photos of potholes and send them in to the council. We attend all the council meetings in order to keep abreast of progress, and so far we are winning hands down. Of course the council officials don't know that we are there, they can't see us. The poor council workers groan when the potholes are counted up and allocated for action, but for us the growing numbers are cause for celebration, and we get extra team points for especially big or disruptive potholes.

I think that one of the best potholes I ever had, which earned me a great deal of respect and was particularly tasty, was on a quiet side road surprisingly. Usually it's the ones on the busy roads that cause the most disruption, especially if we can manage to open one up at the side of a grid, or one of those inspection plates, or make one that disrupts a sewer, although those don't always smell so good. They cause great fun as the council workers, and the public panic about what may be unleashed. Little do they know that the original woman Pandora, with her broken bowl, did the worst unleashing possible all those years ago.

This particular pothole had opened up near the middle of this quiet road through an estate of houses. It is what I think they call a *rat-run*, and a few years ago the council closed it to through traffic, so that only vehicles which belonged there or who were visiting properties in that road should be driving along it.

It didn't work of course, people still used the

rat-run as a short cut and it was there that the pothole opened up. On the day in question it had filled with rainwater the previous night, then there was a heavy frost in the early hours of the morning, and it was not possible for drivers to differentiate between the road surface and the hole. I wish I'd been there to see it, but these days I cover an enormous area and I was scheduled to visit it the following week. As soon as the alarm off went I knew we had scored a hit! Sorry, I mean I knew that some poor driver had fallen foul of a pothole, and I dashed over to take a look. The car was still there. It was a posh one, it was expensive and it seemed to be gushing water from underneath the front – the radiator is it called?

  The driver was still there too, and he was very unhappy. His face had turned a most peculiar colour and he was pacing up and down the footpath talking angrily into his phone. Two of the local residents were standing by their gates chatting about him, so I joined them to eavesdrop. He had, so they said, been driving far too fast and was cutting through their road to avoid congestion elsewhere. Karma they called it. And, best by far was that I scored a hubcap bonus. These used to be very rare, but are more frequent now. They still bring an amount of kudos, and this hubcap had not just come free from its moorings, it had shattered as well, which brings extra points.

  I went back once the car had been removed to make an assessment of the hole. It was one of my better ones, not terribly wide but it was very deep, and the edges were lovely and crumbly. I went back the next day too and, sure enough, it was already patched. I gave the edges a bit of push and found that they moved easily enough; that patch would not be there very long. It was getting on for lunchtime, so I had a bit of a nibble around the edge of it. I broke some bits off and pushed them into the gutter for later. I waited until a car came past and had another look. Yes, more bits of the edging were breaking off already. My work here was done; this hole would re-dig itself.

As well as the weather and the trees, the cable-layers help us. It used to be just telephone cables, and water and gas, but now we seem to need all these wires laid under the roads in order to be wireless! No, I don't understand it either, but it does mean that there are lots of narrow trenches dug along the roads, and across the roads, every inch of which is potential for mischief from us as Gremlins. These people may be experts at laying cables or whatever, but their attempts at digging and filling in trenches are very amateur. Our work is never ending, and we are becoming better known.

Yesterday I saw a headline on a local newspaper that read: 'Pothole opens up on major road, the authorities are looking into it.' Then there was a photograph of all these people stood round looking in this hole. We had a good laugh about that at our team meeting I can tell you.

But there is one more exciting development that I must tell you about. I love the team meetings, and yesterday's I enjoyed a lot. I received applause like you wouldn't believe from my fellow Pans. There had been a particularly difficult drain cover in a major road into the city. The asphalt was loosening quite nicely around the edges as the heavy goods vehicles and buses drove over it regularly. I had a little nibble every time I went past, but it seemed to be taking a long time to break down sufficiently to cause motorists a real nuisance, and I was lucky enough to be checking it out just as a particularly big beast – a tanker with so many wheels you lost count – drove across it. One of the wheels must have hit the drain cover right on the corner. The metal split; one corner sprang up and pierced the vehicle's front tyre with a bang as it slewed all over the road before the driver could come to a halt. The driver was fine; cross but fine. It gladdened my heart (or it would if I had one) to see the mayhem it caused. There were cars swerving this way and that to avoid the tanker. The hole in the road was alarmingly large, especially when part of the drain cover fell down into it. The road had to be closed for repairs, and I was given my second ever standing ovation at the meeting.

      We seldom manage to have road closures on main roads. Unless the pothole is on the white lines, or an accident is caused, then usually they just close it temporarily, then guide the traffic round it. That was what happened in this case. Firstly the road was completely closed to shift the vehicles, and there were temporary lights put up whilst the hole was repaired. I was hoping it may take longer and get a mention on the traffic news on the radio, but they did it quite quickly and by the next morning the traffic lights were gone.

      Then one of our members updated us with some wonderful news from the latest council meeting. The council members had learned, to their dismay and our delight, that there was going to be a big push in the next ten or fifteen years to change to electrically-powered vehicles and, wait for it, these vehicles are on average a third again as heavy as the cars that use the roads at the moment.

It's marvellous news. It'll make such a big difference to the weight of HGV's. All that extra weight on some of these potholes will make it so much easier for us. I foresee a time when potholes and their repairs become a self-managed situation and our services will no longer be needed. The potholes will keep growing themselves and we may even be able to retire back through one of them to our old kingdom, from which we were released all those years ago.

Oh! There goes the alarm letting me know I have another success. Let's check the map. Oh, yes! I've been watching this patch for a while. It's nearly two years now since they dug right across Green Lane, which is a very busy road, to lay cables. Gradually the edges of the excavated channel have been breaking down, and I noticed only a couple of weeks ago that there was some cracking where the channel met the drain inspection cover.

Sorry, I have to go. This one could be a biggy. A Gremlin's work is never done.

Caroline's Cart

Sixteen years ago little Caroline Long from Alabama was just seven years old, when she became the inspiration for her mother's invention, Caroline's Cart. Caroline suffers from Rett Syndrome, a nervous system disorder that causes multiple disabilities.

She loves nothing better than to go out and about to the shops with her mother, Drew. Drew is an inventor and stay-at-home mum living in their home city of Alabaster. She realised that at seven years old, Caroline would soon be too big to lift into conventional child trolleys for use in supermarkets, and that her increasing weight would destabilise such a trolley. Asking what alternatives were available, her local supermarket could offer a manual wheelchair, with a shopping basket attached between the handles. It was usable, but hardly practical for a big family shop. An alternative was a buggy, of the kind used both in the US and the UK by elderly people with mobility problems, but these require certain motor skills that were beyond Caroline's ability. Manoeuvring Caroline single-handedly was becoming too difficult to want to shop several times a week, which would have been necessary when using her manual chair, given the small capacity of the basket. If she had the capacity to fill a trolley, then Drew could make a weekly adventure of the shopping expeditions that gave her daughter so much pleasure.

So Drew set to and designed a suitable cart that could be used from the time a toddler outgrew the conventional shopping trolleys with child seats, right through until adulthood. Wanzl in the USA took up the patent and put the cart into production in 2012. It is suitable for four year olds and above, with a weight limit of 250 lbs, (17 stones 12 pounds) including the shopping. A second child can be accommodated in the cart, and there are sturdy handles on either side, that will support more than eight full shopping bags. The weight limit makes it suitable also for adults. Why should they miss out on shopping trips? The long wheelbase incorporates a footplate and the six-wheel trolley base provides stability and strength.

In 2013 Target commissioned the mass production of Caroline's Cart, with Walmart and Lowe's also interested in the US. Individual managers of Walmart stores are able to order a cart, should they so wish.

Drew Long is not happy to rest on her laurels. She is busy promoting the use of the Caroline's Cart across the US and as far away as Australia and New Zealand to any retail outlets that use shopping trolleys. Even today there is not the amount of penetration into stores that she would like. Cost is no doubt a prohibiting factor, but stores are making their goods inaccessible to a huge raft of potential customers.

There is now a Caroline's Cart Facebook page based in Drew and Caroline's home town in Alabama, aimed at spreading the word.

Michelle Obama heard about Drew's efforts and invited her to visit the White House. The two women spent some time talking about the cart. The First Lady loved the idea, and asked, 'Why do Moms always come up with the best ideas?' Good question.

I suspect that's because usually, although not always, it is a 'Mom' who is required to balance the disabled child that won't fit in a regular trolley, the shopping that won't fit in her regular wheelchair, as well as any other children the family may have.

Hopefully the idea of the carts will continue to gain mileage and spread to other shops and stores around the world.

The Coffee Bean

The shopping and other errands had taken less time than Belle had anticipated and they were nearly home by noon. There was no chance that Evan would have forgotten that he had been promised lunch in a café if he was a good boy while Mummy did what needed doing, and so she pulled into a local service road. This fronted a row of houses, and five shops, the centre one of which was a small café, The Coffee Bean.

Outside the café were a couple of sets of garden furniture, wooden, not the most comfortable and damp from the overnight rain. Belle steered Evan past these and in through the door, which bore a large sign *No Dogs Allowed*. Inside it was warm and cosy. The interior was neat and clean, and the café boasted a limited but adequate menu. At the front, next to the large picture window, was an arrangement of sofas and low tables. It looked very enticing but Evan was still young enough that sitting on an upright chair at a higher table was less likely to end in spillages. They made their way past the halfway point, where the counter projected into the room, and settled themselves at a table backing onto the side wall.

A group of ladies who had been seated on the comfortable seats left the café as they entered, leaving just one person sitting right at the back. She sat under a small window, which showed a tiny courtyard beyond. She was drinking a mug of coffee and was engrossed in the book she was reading.

Before she finished work to concentrate on bringing up her family, Belle had worked in industry, her job involving her in visiting companies of all sizes, advising them on areas where they could improve their business. She was particularly enthusiastic about small businesses such as The Coffee Bean and helping them to make the most of their assets. Whenever she entered anywhere like this it was impossible for Belle to take off her adviser's head, and she immediately spotted a number of areas where the place could be made more attractive; not in terms of looking prettier, but more in terms of general appeal and functionality to improve profits.

Probably because it was so quiet, in spite of being lunchtime, the owner was inclined to chat. She brought over their plain cheese toasties and Evan immediately tucked in. Between mouthfuls he began, 'if you want, my Mummy will make more people come to your café. There's nearly nobody here.'

Belle almost choked, 'Evan, please don't be rude. The lady knows how to run her business. You just eat your toastie if you want one of those scrummy-looking puddings over there.'

The proprietor sat down, 'I'm always ready to listen to suggestions if there are ways we can improve. I'm happy to take on new ideas.'

'There are a few things I'd change I suppose, but it's really none of my business,' Belle was cagey. There was quite a lot she could see that would make a difference.

The proprietor was getting a bit huffy now, 'No. You tell me what you think.'

'Okay,' Belle took a deep breath. 'I always try to think of impact on the bottom line. I wouldn't suggest that your business needs any expensive input. The tiled floor and the furniture are lovely and modern, and you obviously keep everything beautifully clean. The notice on the door that dogs are only allowed outside is something I would change.'

The woman, so keen to have Belle's opinion a moment ago, was beginning to look cross. 'I can't have dogs pushing past all the expensive sofas, shaking themselves, possibly having lifting their legs against the furniture.' She shook her head emphatically, but Belle had expected resistance.

'Okay,' she said, 'it's only an idea. At the moment dogs have to stay outside, I see you have water for them out there, which is great, but I suspect most people won't want to sit outside when it rains. Even when the weather's lovely people would be sitting in full sun – quite hot for dogs to be in for long, and the main road is just metres away. Nothing is going to change that.'

She paused and wiped Evan's face, and waited while he chose his ice-cream dessert.

'As for dogs pushing past the sofas, I would swap the two areas around. I would put the sofas and low tables under the back window, and put some inexpensive bookshelves behind them. I would put all the practical, washable tables and chairs in the front window, put the dog water bowl in there, and a sign on the end of the counter: *No dogs past this point please.* Many people acquired dogs during the lockdown, and not being able to take them inside somewhere I suspect is drastically reducing your appeal for those people.'

A shake of the head showed Belle that she was not getting anywhere with the dogs, so she tried a different aspect. 'The bookshelves I would fill with paperbacks; they are very cheap in charity shops and you could suggest that people can enjoy them while they wait for their friends, they can donate books of their own and buy those on display if they wish. You could donate the proceeds to a charity.'

'But giving money away to a charity isn't going to increase my profits.'

'It's about increasing your footfall. Someone paying fifty pence or a pound for a paperback book is going to spend considerably more on coffees or lunch. They will also tell their friends about you; maybe use The Coffee Bean as a place to meet those friends; start to become regular customers.' Belle looked pointedly around the near-empty premises, 'It's lunchtime and you need to encourage more people in perhaps.'

The proprietor looked unconvinced, 'What about the food. What's wrong with that?'

'The food was delicious, although we only had a toastie of course. Evan, is the pudding good?'

'Brilliant,' he said through an ice cream smile.

'My only suggestion,' Belle said, 'might be a little garnish on the food. A halved cherry tomato and a lettuce leaf would make a deal of difference to the presentation of the toasties. I see that you have a little yard out there at the back. You'd only need a growbag, or hanging baskets and a couple of packets of seeds. You could maybe let children look through the window, and choose their own tomato to be sliced on their sandwich. Anyway, we must be going now. I'll have the bill please.'

As they reached the counter to pay, the other woman who had been sitting at the back of the café was also paying for her single cup of coffee. When the proprietor was out of earshot she leaned over to Belle.

'You're quite right,' she told her. 'She could do so much more, but she's stubborn, she won't be told.'

It was twelve months before Belle passed that way again in the car. Not totally unexpected was the sight that greeted her. The café was closed up, a *To Let* sign in the window. What a shame; for the sake of a couple of MDF shelves and hanging baskets, then moving the furniture round.

Would her ideas have saved The Coffee Bean if they'd been implemented straight away? Perhaps not, what was really needed was a change of mindset, but there was no way of knowing now.

Or was there? Belle passed down that road a few months later, and her eye was caught by strings of brightly coloured fairy lights strung across the windows. Underneath was a brightly coloured sign: *Dogs Welcome!* alongside another sign which read *Under New Management.*

Curiosity getting the better of her, she parked her car and went inside. At the front of the café area was the washable furniture that had been at the back, and two families, accompanied by their dogs, were chatting happily. As she went through to the rear of the shop she could see that all the changes she had recommended had been actioned.

On the comfortable sofas, arranged just as she had suggested, was a group of women discussing books they had on the coffee tables in front of them. By the number of empty mugs on the tables they had been there for some time. The new proprietor of the shop was talking to them: 'Right girls, let's have your lunch orders, otherwise I won't have time to serve you when the rush begins. If you're keeping any of the books please pop your contribution into the charity tin on the counter.'

Two of the ladies took books with them, and made their payment on the way out. The others gave the owner their lunch orders. As she stood, Belle could see a small garden through the window – exactly as she had recommended. There were cut-and-come-again lettuces, cherry tomatoes, borage and nasturtiums, flowers from which were used on the ice cream counter to enhance the display.

At last the owner turned around as the cheerful shop's bell rang out as more customers entered. She spotted Belle. It was the lady who had been sitting reading on her own at the back of the café when Belle and Evan had first been in.

'I've been so hoping that you'd come back,' she said, 'it was so obvious that you had some really good ideas for this place and that other woman wasn't prepared to listen. As soon as I heard it was empty I came and made a bid. We're going from strength to strength. I hope you like what we've done with it.' She lowered her voice: 'The cake shop next door may be coming on the market soon as the owner is retiring. We may even be expanding.

'I have some really great ideas for that area if

we're able to take it over. I have my eye on a sixties ice cream machine, and plans for a take-away area, all sorts of things. I'd love to tell you all about it but I need to serve these customers.

Belle laughed, 'I think you've implemented everything I said at the time. Of course I like it. You deserve to do well. I'll come back in a few weeks. I'll bring Evan for lunch again and see how you're getting on.' The owner turned to a girl who had come out from the kitchen to help serve the influx of customers.

'This lady gets free coffee and food whenever she comes in,' she told her. 'Without her input I doubt I'd even have looked at this place. We have a lot to be grateful for.'

Hole in One

GOLF CLUB OPEN DAY PLANNING COMMITTEE MEETING, FEBRUARY

Chairman: 'Agenda Item 4. It is proposed that changes be made to the tombola at the next Open Day, for the benefit of other club members and visitors. The two ladies who run the tombola stall were once again put in an awkward position because a certain honorary member of the club bought up so many strips of tombola tickets immediately on the event opening at 10 o'clock, that he was bound to win some of the more substantial prizes before anyone else had even seen them. The same person then returned several times to the tombola and bought more tickets.'

From the Floor: 'You don't need to beat about the bush. We all know you're talking about Jeff Merton. He does it every year.'

From the Floor: 'He got some good prizes last time, but members who had either played a round of golf before coming into the club house, or visitors who came later complained that there was little left by lunchtime. The open day is supposed to be an opportunity to bring in new members, especially youngsters, but seeing that sort of behaviour from members must be very off-putting.'

Chairman: 'Exactly. My proposal is that club members may not buy tombola tickets until 12 noon, so giving others a chance.'

From the Floor: 'That seems somewhat draconian.'

Chairman: 'It might do, but consider this from the last open day. There was a large red fire engine, new, in its box which had been donated as a tombola prize by a local company, and one little boy really wanted it. His family spent a lot on tickets, at least as much as Jeff, and he kept coming back and back. In the end he got it but only because the ladies, with the approval of the Club chairman I might add, switched tickets to make sure his next ticket 'won' it. Jeff was annoyed: he had really wanted it too, he said that he had bought lots of tickets, it wasn't fair – like a petulant child.'

From the Floor: 'Well it wasn't fair was it really? Everyone should have an equal chance.'

Chairman: 'No, in a way it wasn't fair, but consider this. Jeff won four or five prizes each with a value of over £10, so he did okay, as well as some smaller stuff. Next day I checked on social media and on-line auctions, and all of those items were for sale at well above £10 each. By the end of the week they had all sold and Jeff had made £50 or so profit on his tombola tickets. One purpose of the Open Day tombola is to raise money for a local charity and I feel that Jeff was ripping off not only a small child, but also the charity.'

From the Floor: 'Apologies, but as a new

member I don't think I have yet met Jeff. I'm assuming he is a member here?'

Chairman: 'Jeff is a bookkeeper ...'

From the Floor: 'A bookkeeper who told us that he was an accountant although he is unqualified.'

Chairman: 'Indeed. He had offered to keep the club accounts in exchange for *the odd game or two*. He had been offered and accepted, honorary membership of the club in exchange for managing the accounts.'

From the Floor: 'Aye, but his *odd game or two* has now morphed into a regular appearance on the first tee every weekend.'

After further discussion a vote was held: CARRIED UNANIMOUSLY.

* * *

*GOLF CLUB ANNUAL GENERAL MEETING, MAY *

At the AGM the new rules for the upcoming Open Day tombola stall had been announced. No vote was needed as the members of the Open Day Planning Committee were the decision-makers. In any event Jeff Merton, as an honorary club member, would have no vote. That didn't stop him from loudly voicing his objections. He finished his childish strop by telling the assembled company what they could do with their tin-pot golf club, as he had been offered full membership at the much more prestigious Queen Mary's Club across town, although many members doubted this. He made to gather up the papers in front of him, but the Chair intervened. 'Are we to accept this as your resignation Jeff?'

When Jeff confirmed this the Chair insisted that, as the accounts and related documents belonged to the club, these be left behind. Jeff tried to backtrack, but a vote immediately resulted in the unanimous acceptance of his resignation and he had no choice but to leave.

* * *

GOLF CLUB EXTRAORDINARY MEETING OF THE FINANCE COMMITTEE, JULY

In attendance: The Golf Club Chairman; the Open Day Committee Chairman; the Representative of the newly appointed Accountancy firm; and a further quorum of club members.

Club Chairman: I have called this extraordinary meeting in part to introduce Mr Callaghan, from the firm of Griffith Londson, who have been appointed as our accountants after Jeff's departure. There are however some things that have come to light, both by Mr Callaghan examining the accounts and by several club members, that require discussion and possibly need further investigation.'

Mr Callaghan: 'You all have a copy of the latest accounts and I have highlighted two or three entries. By and large the accounts are fine and are in order, matching the balance held in the two bank accounts in the club's name. I would draw your attention firstly to the area circled in red, and numbered (1). There is missing from between those two amounts, a third amount that was received by Mr Merton on behalf of the club. I have carried out a complete audit and the sum, received as cash paid for green fees in the previous quarter has never been entered in the accounts. Nor has the amount, some £250 been paid into the bank.

'Also last year's tombola fund, which the ladies totted up on the day before handing it to Mr Merton; their recollection is that there was some £120 in cash. That amount was never paid in either; it should be listed between the refreshments profit, and the admission fees as shown by number (2) on the second sheet. The previous year's tombola and refreshment monies were submitted, although informally the tombola ladies and those serving teas feel that the amount should have been greater. It is not my position to speculate, but in each case it is cash that may have gone missing. I suspect that maybe two sets of books were kept, and that once Jeff had signed off the accounts, he could then hang onto the cash not accounted for, or suddenly *find* it and pay it into the bank if anybody queried it. He also signed off the accounts as if he still worked for an accountancy firm in the city. Some digging showed that he had worked their briefly inputting VAT data, but that he was not and never had been qualified.'

Club Chairman: 'So what recourse do we have? How can we get money back that has been ...'

Mr Callaghan: 'Stolen is the word Mr Chairman. With Mr Merton the only one who dealt with the accounts, it is difficult. Incidentally he signed off the accounts as accurate for each of the last three years that he has been working with you. He is not qualified to do that. Only a qualified accountant currently working in the sector can sign off the accounts as accurate, Mr Merton never was qualified as an accountant.'

Open Day Committee Chairman: 'But some of that money was for charity, and some for the upkeep of the club and greens. Is there nothing we can do?'

Mr Callaghan: 'There is, but it will mean involving the police. The two tombola ladies, and the refreshments ladies may be required to attend court and give evidence. It is not a pleasant experience for anyone involved. We have a trail of sorts, in that Jeff himself contributed to the tombola takings, and a court would I think look positively on your case, given that he immediately sold four items identical to the prizes people witnessed him winning. That audit trail is intact. With money from the refreshments, it is more difficult to prove, although many people can verify that they were served refreshments that day, and handed over money in exchange. So there definitely should be some money and we should be able to estimate how much. It may rely though on people being prepared and able to stand up in court and confirm what they are saying in private.'

Club Chairman: 'There is one other thing. In preparation for today's meeting I have been talking in confidence to a few club members, people who had identified themselves as concerned already about Jeff. Two told me that he had approached them to see if they could make a donation towards replacement windows in the club bar. He told them that without sufficient funds the clubhouse may have to close as it could be unsafe. He suggested that the bar area would probably be named after any patron who donated. A third member told me that his elderly mother had been approached with the same story. Her late husband was Club Chairman for many years and in his name she was persuaded to part with six thousand pounds.

'Their son is a member here, and he has said that he is prepared to push this as far as necessary. His mother had told him that she was making provision for a donation to the golf club, and he had thought nothing of it, thinking she was referring to her will. She is very old and may not be able to appear in court, but we need to involve the police in order that they take down her statement, and the son's. Mr Callaghan confirmed to me that no amount of six thousand pounds appears anywhere in the accounts. The police will apparently be able to get a court order to search any bank accounts Jeff has or had at the time, to see where the money went. The old lady gave him a cheque, which was cleared by her bank a few days later, so there should be a clear audit trail there. Incidentally, there is absolutely nothing wrong with the club bar windows.

* * *

THE OUTCOME, CROWN COURT, MAY

It took ten months for Jeff Merton to be tracked down, the necessary papers served and searches made. Sadly in the meantime the old lady who played such a large part in his criminal demise passed away. Although, as her son said on leaving the court after sentence was passed down, it was perhaps a blessing that she never knew how she had been deceived. Jeff was found guilty, sentenced to pay costs, repay the golf club a total of seven thousand, three hundred pounds, and to three years in prison for embezzlement and false accounting. He would come out of prison to find that his home had been sold to repay the debt, and his wife had taken their only child to live with her parents in the USA. With a criminal record it was doubtful that Jeff would be allowed to visit.

It made the Club Chairman wonder whether Jeff believed it was worth it, and whether, if he hadn't been quite so cocky about the tombola tickets, he may have got away with it all.

First Date

It's my birthday today. I'm eighty-eight. Although up until a few minutes ago I had that wrong.

We had moved house in 1940, wartime of course and I can't remember much of my life before that. I certainly don't remember going to school at the old place, and am pretty sure that it was after our move that I went to school for the first time. My dad was involved in national gas supplies, and so was in a reserved occupation. The house move was partly to be nearer to the Gas Works where he was employed I think. He must have been fairly important; I remember that years later the Gas Board fitted a telephone in our hallway, so he could be reached in an emergency. Previously they had had to send a motorbike courier if he was needed on site out of hours. The telephone engineer asked my mother whether she wanted to call someone to try the new phone out, but she had to tell him that she didn't know of anyone else who had a phone, so she couldn't. I recall her telling that story again and again over the years.

I remember that in 1940 we moved, not into the house itself, but into the cellar. Of course for a little girl of my age it was more exciting than frightening, and we would listen to the blitz over Manchester by night and watch the lights across the sky through the opening to the coal chute. Later there were doodlebugs that caused considerable damage in the area, but that was not till 1944.

The cellar was invaluable in that there was no need for us to decamp to the air-raid shelter at the end of the street when the air raid sirens went off. Sometimes the neighbours or passers-by would come into us, rather than spend more time than was necessary outside.

My sister Margery was ten years older than me, and she was at work each day; something based at the nearby Ringway Airport, but she wasn't allowed to tell us what. She and my parents are all gone now, so there's nobody to explain to me the puzzle that I've just discovered.

There wasn't a particular reason why I was going through the box this morning, other than it is my birthday. This box is where I keep important things and treasures. Whatever the reason, I came across the sheaf of certificates and there, on top, was my birth certificate. I looked at it for the first time in years, and noticed something bizarre that I'd never noticed before.

'Pamela,' I said to myself, sitting on the bed, clutching the document, 'This can't possibly be right.'

And yet here it is, my original birth certificate, duly signed, with a postage stamp in the bottom right hand corner, which the officiating Registrar had signed across. That was how they did it then, the original one penny stamp duty to authorise an official document. I looked at Margery's certificate, and those of our parents. All had a similar stamp and a signature across the bottom right.

I looked again at my own. It clearly gave my date of birth as 1935, and the Registrar had dated the document itself a few days later, presumably when my birth was actually registered. All this time I have believed that I was born in 1936, exactly ten years after my sister. I could clearly remember my mother telling people time and again that there was a ten year age gap between the two of us. And yet there wasn't, was there? My sister was born in 1926, and this official document clearly stated that I was born in 1935. Because my mum used to say that it was ten years, I think she must have used the incorrect age from me being quite young.

Below the certificates in my box is a metallic *21* cake topper, saved from my coming-of-age birthday cake. But it wasn't my coming-of-age was it? That had really happened the year before. It was the same with my fiftieth birthday party and, just a few years ago, my eightieth. My children and grandchildren had clubbed together and we had gone out for a meal. There were balloons with 80 on them, and a cake with candles spelling out 80. All the restaurant staff and clients had cheered and sang happy birthday, and it was all wrong.

And now my problem is: does it matter? I have long retired, and anyway my pension is as a result of my late husband's employment, so that is not an issue. I have never learned to drive, so no false claims had been made there. I have travelled abroad many times. Presumably the date on my passport had never been checked, although why would it be questioned? Who can accurately tell the difference between a forty year old and a forty one year old? As I was totally oblivious to the problem, I wouldn't have looked shifty, or as if I had anything to hide; otherwise I suppose I might have been challenged.

What I do need to do now is get onto the GP surgery, and my dentist, and make sure that the family know the story, although what need they would have for that information I had no idea.

It has set me wondering though, and this afternoon I had a chat with a friend, who is a similar sort of age to me. She told me that her mother had talked a lot about the time when she started school. She said her mother simply went down to the school when she was about four and a half and told them her name, address and age. They then sent for her to start school once she passed her fifth birthday. There was no immunisation for children in those days; vaccines for mumps, measles, rubella and polio not being developed until a lot later. Most male teachers had been called up to fight, and a large number of retired female teachers came back into teaching to fill the gap.

The NHS was not launched until 1948, so doctors had to be paid for their services, and home remedies were always the first resort, before paying for anything medical. There was certainly none of the 'cradle to the grave' care and monitoring that there would be today. On starting school there were none of the checks and balances that youngsters undergo these days; no pre-school checks, no health officials to suggest that you were big or small for your age, or that you were advanced or struggling compared with your year group, or that you were due for this inoculation or that one. Your mum was asked for your date of birth, and that was it. Whatever she said pretty much became your date of birth.

I have two grown-up children, but both were home births, so again there was no documentation concerning me during the process. Nobody that I can recall questioned my birth date at any stage of my life.

So here I am, at eighty-eight, and none the worse for the mistake made all those years ago, and perpetuated ever since. It does make me wonder how many other old people may have been in the same situation. My sister and I were the only children in our family, but in big families – my mother was one of seven – it must have been very easy to make such a mistake, and with little opportunity or need to put it right.

I tucked the cake topper and the certificates back into the box. Nothing has changed. I am still the same person I believed myself to be, just a year older. That's all.

The Switch

Like many Londoners, Alfie always found the morning commute to be the worst part of his day. He enjoyed his job, but not having to fight through the crowds, and cope with the underground car getting fuller and fuller, until it seemed that not another person could squeeze through the doors. Getting a seat, which he often could as he entered the train at Cockfosters, the northernmost end of the Piccadilly Line, was a mixed blessing. On one hand it avoided the threat of being knocked off his feet at every jolt, but when it came time to disembark, it was always a struggle to get up and fight his way to the door.

On this particular morning Alfie had secured a window seat, forward facing and not too far from the doors. There were several women, mostly young women, having to stand for the journey that morning, but it was impractical to offer any of them a seat. It would require climbing over other people, and would cause more disruption than it was worth for a fairly short journey. He made eye contact with one young lady, who shook her head at him. She must have agreed that the effort was not worth it. He held her look for a long moment. She had the most remarkable eyes, hazel but the left was flecked with gold. Around the iris were flecks of different pigment. It was most unusual. It was only when she cocked her head to one side and raised her eyebrows at him that he realised he was staring, and looked away. She picked up her bag and shuffled down the aisle as yet more people joined the train at Oakwood Station and the train continued its journey south towards the city centre.

To hide his embarrassment Alfie took out his book and was lost in the George Saunders story when the tannoy crackled and a disembodied voice made an announcement that no London commuter ever wants to hear: *'Ladies and Gentlemen, due to a signalling failure, this service will now terminate at Southgate Station. Repeat, this service will terminate at Southgate Station due to a signalling failure. Please make sure that you have all your belongings with you on leaving the train.'*

A chorus of tutting and groaning followed. People suddenly began to shuffle around, check their watches and to speak into their phones, no doubt pre-emptively explaining their lateness. Alfie was not unduly worried. There would be plenty of buses from Station Parade at Southgate, but they would more than double, probably treble his journey time to Kings Cross, especially as this train debouched its cargo of humanity and it seemed that everybody else also headed up the stairs to the bus depot. Alfie's backpack had been kicked along the aisle slightly as the mass of disgruntled passengers moved towards the door, and eventually the young lady he had made eye contact with earlier paused to give him the opportunity to leave his seat. He smiled his thanks as she slung her backpack over one shoulder, her handbag over the other, and was carried away in the throng of people pushing forward. He tucked his paperback in the front pocket of his backpack and made his way to the Parade. Most of the commuters had had the same idea. A few had rushed to the taxi rank, but with a half hour journey still ahead, Alfie supposed that for many commuters, the cost of this would perhaps be a problem.

  The bus was packed. He shoved his backpack between his feet as it began to jolt its way down High Street. The journey took longer even than Alfie had anticipated, stopping at every bus stop along the route. Eventually it approached Kings Cross Station a full hour and a half later than he had planned, but he still wasn't too concerned. The Eurostar wouldn't leave until midday from St Pancras Station, just across the road. He would still have plenty of time to reach the Paris office for his afternoon meeting.

  It was as Alfie swung his backpack across his shoulder that he noticed that the straps seemed very tight, they seemed shorter than before. He dropped it to the ground again, and noticed how scruffy it was looking. He had not noticed that before. Then he saw the scrawls of red marks across the back of it; as if he had brushed it up against something. Was it paint, or felt tip? Something like that, and then the reality dawned.

  This backpack, a common make and style from a national sportswear shop with branches on every high street, was not his. He looked around in a panic, but no similar backpack was in sight. He watched as the bus now headed off down the busy road, too far to chase after, even if he could have been sure of his own possessions being on board. He thought back, wondering how and when this could have happened. This bag was shabbier, older than his own. At some point, maybe on the train, or on the bus he had picked up the wrong backpack and presumably someone else had wrongly picked up his. The paperback he had tucked into the front pocket was still there, which would suggest that he had been carrying this one since the train stopped at Southgate at least, and he now had no idea of the whereabouts of his own. It could be anywhere. He stopped on the footpath, holding up others trying to pass. Perhaps he was wrong; although of course he knew it wasn't his, he checked anyway.

Moving into the St Pancras station concourse, he found a bench where he could examine the contents. Another paperback was tucked inside. It looked interesting, but why was he bothering about this stranger's stuff? Without his own backpack he would be going nowhere. All his travel documents were in there, as well as his clothes. He needed to find out who owned this backpack and just hope that they had picked his up in error. He glanced at the clock; he knew that he could transfer to a later Eurostar train. A more pressing issue was that he had nothing to prove he had booked the Eurostar. He had no ticket, no passport, nothing, and he had a three o'clock meeting to attend in Paris. Thank goodness his wallet was in his pocket. He bought himself a cup of coffee, and started to search the stranger's bag for clues.

It contained no phone, no laptop or tablet, no money or ID. The owner must keep those separately. Only a folder of closely written text, stories they looked like, grouped together in a folder with the name Mina C scribbled on the flyleaf. It seemed to be a story or a group of stories: about life in a wartime town in England somewhere. There were descriptions of back alleyways behind terraced houses, children going to collect a container of milk from a local farm, maybe a dozen or more stories, and each story or section was accompanied by a very competently drawn pencil sketch. There were children playing hopscotch in the street; a little boy aiming a catapult at a row of cans on the top of a drystone wall, and the most thought-provoking of all a sketch showing the inside of a corner shop, with children choosing sweets from a jar. It looked to Alfie just like the corner shop at the back of the little cluster of streets in Cockfosters known as Little Italy.

There was an illustration of an elderly lady pulling a large open wicker basket on wheels, exactly like the one his grandmother had used. Jemima Puddletruck the children in the family had called it.

But enough of that. This Mina person, who presumably owned the backpack, must have boarded the train at either Cockfosters or Oakwood, but these need not necessarily have been where her journey started. She could have driven and parked up at either station; or travelled that far by bus. There could not, he mused, these days be so many shops just like she had depicted, but it need not necessarily be the one at Cockfosters. It could have been drawn from an old photograph, or some older person's narrative. In any event, even if he could identify the shop, that did not help him today. He began to look through the stories, and soon became immersed.

Mina Curtis had grabbed her shoulder bag and backpack, sprinted across the Southgate station platform and up the steps to jump on the N29 bus for Finsbury Park, where she had a meeting planned with a literary agent. The bus was nearly as crowded as the train had been, and she held both bags clutched across her chest to protect her work from getting damaged. She was pleased with it, the stories of course, but particularly the illustrations that accompanied them. It was a long time since she had done any painting, but she had enjoyed producing these evocative pencil sketches and hoped that the agent would be won over by their simplicity.

She had plenty of time before her meeting with the agent. She had promised her nephew that she would take some photographs of the Hogwarts' portal on King's Cross Station and made her way to the iconic landmark. It wasn't until she went into the coffee shop, putting her arm through the backpack that she thought it seemed very loose. A closer look revealed the terrible truth. This pack was the same as hers but newer, smarter, and, sickeningly, it did not have the rigidity that her folder of work would give it.

She grabbed a cup of coffee beginning to panic now, as she emptied the contents of the stranger's backpack on the table. There was a name on travel documents, and an address. There was a passport, with a photograph of a young man whose face she thought she recognised from the train, but that did not help. It was as she delved into an inner pocket and retrieved a mobile phone, that it began to ring. It was an unknown number, and she hesitated for a moment.

'Hello?' she was tentative. It could be anybody, but yet she had nothing to lose.

'Mina?'

'Yes, but how . . . '

'I'm Alfie. I have your bag, and you must have mine as you've answered my phone. Where are you?'

'Outside the coffee shop at King's Cross Station. You?'

'Just across the road at St Pancras. I'm using one of the bank of telephones there on the back wall. What are you wearing, apart from my backpack?' he laughed, 'I'll be there in five minutes. I had to go through your bag of course, but I just wanted to say I think your stories and illustrations are great. '

Within minutes he found himself looking into the extraordinary eyes of the girl he had seen on the train; the girl with the unusual hazel eyes, one flecked with gold. After each apologising for the mix-up, the two exchanged bags. Alfie had left his untouched coffee across the road at St Pancras. He went to the counter to buy them each another.

They chatted easily but briefly and all too soon Mina gathered her belongings together, 'I must go, wish me luck for this interview.'

'You don't need luck, but good luck anyway.'

Alfie watched her hurry across to the station exit, then checked his bag, ready to go across to the Eurostar terminal. There were his travel documents as he had left them. Tucked inside the front of the passport was a scrap of paper. She must have put it there when he went for their coffees.

On it was written, 'If you really liked my stories and pictures perhaps we could meet up some time, and I can tell you about them, and about my interview? It was signed *Mina,* along with a telephone number.

Alfie found he was looking forward to the meeting in Paris that afternoon, but looking forward even more to getting back home.

Clippety Clop

The social media post was heartfelt: 'Please don't message me any more about the horses running free on the lane in Earsby Village. I have done all I can to help and keep getting abuse to the extent that it's grinding me down. The horses are nothing to do with me. The field from which they keep escaping is on my route to work, that is all. I have spoken to the owner, to receive nothing but abuse, and also to the police about them and posted on here several times, but I repeat – THE HORSES ARE NOTHING TO DO WITH ME, other than I've tried to be a good citizen and prevent an accident to them and to passing traffic. If you're concerned about their welfare I suggest that you contact either the police or the RSPCA.'

Freya re-read what she had written, considered it harsh but hit send anyway. This whole situation had got out of hand, and was affecting her mental health. Her mother, who had advised her from the start to stay out of it, said that it was driving her crazy, and she wasn't far wrong. Several times she had woken in the night in a panic about the horses, one of them getting out and falling off the old railway bridge alongside their field, following the lane as far as the motorway junction, or simply getting hit by a car on the lane: the consequences of which didn't bear thinking about.

Twice already she had become involved and although even as she was having second thoughts about the wording of her post, she had neither the time nor the strength to continue this fight. As she understood things the lease on the field where the two horses grazed was not to be renewed. Green belt or not, the land was being sold off for development, and the field's owner was no longer prepared to spend money on maintenance of the fences and gate. It seems that the horses' owner who rented the field was losing interest in them too. She lived some distance away and rarely visited. Twice Freya had driven past the field in recent weeks and there had been virtually no water in the trough and the food stand had been empty. After a wet autumn the ground was muddy, with only the odd tuft of grass here and there for the horses to eat. Their coats were shaggy and matted. They hadn't been groomed in a long time.

Freya loved horses and hated to see these suffering but, although Earsby Manor, where she and her mother lived, was large with several paddocks and fields around it, the cost of its upkeep was so high that there was little money left for anything else. She and her mother had not been on holiday for three years and could not commit the money that would be needed to properly look after the horses were they to make some sort of rescue bid.

After work, unsettled by the whole situation, and particularly by some of the unkind responses she came home to on social media, she went out for a walk down the fields belonging to Earsby Manor. In fact two of the fields were quite well fenced and would do admirably to house the horses in the summer months, but come winter she would struggle. Then the horses would need hay buying in once the grass was no longer viable, and they would need some sort of shelter. There could potentially be hefty vet bills as well. It just didn't seem practical. She wandered on, to the boundary where the manor's land ended at the canal.

She had the *Peaceful Princess,* moored on the canal, but selling an old narrow boat, watertight and cosy though she was, would hardly raise enough money to help. Keeping horses is an expensive pastime. Perhaps she could think of something else.

The idea came to her in the early hours of the following morning. It could work, it could work very well. But what would her mother make of it? She waited several days, unsure how to raise her thoughts, but an opening came when the gas bill arrived. As usual it seemed extortionate. The manor was old, draughty and very large. Keeping it at a remotely liveable temperature cost a fortune.

'I don't think we can stay here, Freya,' said her mother, 'the upkeep is simply too high, and it's far too big now that there are just the two of us rattling around in it.'

It was the straw Freya needed and she clutched at it. 'I know. I've even wondered whether we could manage on the boat and sell the manor off. We've had property developers after it before to turn it into flats. Maybe we should look into it.'

She was surprised at her mother's immediate

response, 'I think we should. There's an awful lot of furniture and things that could be sold off too, but I bet you'd like to keep some of the fields and paddocks so you can rescue those horses. I know they've been on your mind.'

Freya flung her arms around her mother, 'They have, and if we lived on the boat we'd be right on the spot to look after them.'

They set about planning with the help of an old map which fields would be best kept for the horses; then explored how to go about registering a rescue charity and other details. By the afternoon they had arranged a meeting with their solicitor and had looked out old letters they had received from a couple of hotel chains and a property developer who had each expressed an interest in the manor. If they could get a bidding war going, then they should be able to raise a good sum.

In the meantime the two horses were still in an unsafe environment, which was giving Freya sleepless nights. She decided to take the bull by the horns, and went to speak to their owner.

'You're the bitch who keeps interfering through social media,' she said, when Freya gave her name. Then she slammed the door in Freya's face, leaving Freya to shout out her plans through the letterbox. The woman only opened the door again and began to engage when she saw that there could be money involved.

'I've had the police on at me, and those animal welfare people and it's all your fault.'

'If you're not in a position to look after them,' Freya carefully avoided suggesting that the woman had grown bored with equine management and wasn't taking proper care of the horses, 'surely it would be better to move them on? I couldn't pay you a lot, but I would buy them off you and guarantee that they would be well looked after.' It needed some tough negotiations, until eventually Freya played her trump card, 'If the RSPCA become involved again, you could be facing a hefty fine – up to £5000 for each animal. Better surely to sell them to me and be done with it.'

Freya didn't want to wait, and went that afternoon to the bank to organise a loan. With the manor house as security, a letter from her solicitor confirming that the property would be on the market imminently, and his approximate valuation, the transaction went smoothly. She couldn't rest easy until the horses were paid for and rehoused in the paddock nearest to the canal. Their previous owner had mellowed somewhat, especially on receiving the bankers' draft, and had also passed on to Freya the horses' tack and the food she had stored in her barn.

It wouldn't last long though, and now that the horses were being given sufficient food they seemed to eat everything they were offered. They began to put on weight and their coats became shinier.

Within months the manor had been bought by an organisation which used such places as bistro hotels. They had no need of most of the fields and paddocks, just a small area immediately adjacent to the building, which they would landscape as gardens, and a car park. They were happy to leave ownership of the two fields and the paddock with Freya and her mother. Before the hotel opened the following winter, they had installed new bathrooms, moving the old bathtubs to the paddock for Freya to use with the horses. They wouldn't care that their drinking troughs were avocado green.

A new wooden stable block had been built close to the boat, and a small covered arena, so that the horses could be ridden in all weather. For Freya had been approached by an organisation wanting to provide riding opportunities for children with disabilities. The hotel also arranged for guests with children to allow them to ride, and help with the horses. Emboldened, Freya gave up her job and focused on the rescue centre full time. There were by now four horses in the rescue fields, three of whom were suitable for children to ride. Freya and her mother had settled onto the boat, finding that the initial cramped feeling was quickly overcome by everything being to hand, and easy and quick to clean. She had plans to go and view a second hand horsebox, and there were two more horses that she had been notified about by the RSPCA.

During bad weather the following winter, the hotel owner invited Freya and her mother to make use of one of their empty bedrooms in preference to the boat, and even their laundry facilities for a token fee as long as they were not used for horse blankets!

In spite of the hard work, and the inevitable ups and downs of working with animals, especially rescue animals, Freya found herself sleeping soundly at night and she was happier and more content than she had ever been.

The Best Friend's Guilt Trip

Let's be quite clear about this, I am not, never was and never could be Mary's best friend. She was an elderly neighbour of mine when the children were small, nothing more. Yet disturbingly, several times, I heard her describe me, in company and once on the phone, as her best friend. *Bestie* she said, trying to be hip and young instead of old and needy, which is what she really was. But don't take my word for it. I may be the one hopelessly out of step here, you judge for yourselves.

I will admit that when the twins were small, she was very helpful, which sounds awful of me, like I'm taking advantage of her problems or her availability or something, but, given her age she no longer went out to work, and so she was always around. When our twins were small we lived directly opposite. She spent a lot of time since she was widowed in her front window, bored I suppose, but it meant that I could hardly ever leave the house without her knowing about it, and she would routinely call out to me about where I was going, when I would be back and so on. There was a fair bit of comment of the *'Oh, I always wanted to go there'* sort of thing, and sometimes it was very difficult not to invite her along.

In those days she was still driving, although in my opinion she shouldn't have been. It's not easy is it, getting that message across to someone without offending them? I certainly didn't manage it with Mary, although one of her oldest friends had long-since refused to go in her car with her at all, so surely the writing was already on the wall. I don't know whether she got all offended at that, but it was not long before her car was due a service, and failed its MOT so at last she let it go.

Often, a couple of times a week I suppose, we would have a coffee together, either at her house or mine, and she would help to keep an eye on the twins for me. Not that I abused that privilege, I hope. I didn't go out shopping or anything. It was just nice to nip to the loo unaccompanied, or into the kitchen to put the kettle on or pop the dinner into the oven. Not a lot to ask of life really and she loved being useful, so I felt it benefitted us both.

There was only one thing that concerned me really, and that was how very unkind she could be. I don't mean unkind in a physical way, I would never have let her near my babies if I had any concerns about that. It was the tongue-lashing sort of unkindness that Mary went in for. She had been born and brought up locally, taking over her parents' house eventually, where she continued to live. Her cruelty was observable in quite a devious way. It was to do with how she spoke about people behind their backs.

Mary's next-door neighbours were very good about taking her shopping once a week. I offered to sort out her shopping on line, but she liked to see what she was getting, squeeze the fruit and check the best before dates. That is understandable, but made it an exhausting trip and one I was glad to get out of because of my commitment to the twins.

Sometimes those same neighbours would go and get specific things on her behalf; things that weren't part of the usual supermarket run that they all did together. But it seemed that the shopping that they kindly brought to her was never quite what she wanted, never quite right. It was either the wrong brand, or bought from the wrong shop, or they had paid too much for it. I get it to a point; it's difficult shopping on someone else's behalf unless you have brand, style, colours specified for you, and even then it's not ideal.

The pensioner next door on the other side of Mary brought round her daily newspaper when she had finished reading it. The visit also meant that she could keep a motherly eye on Mary at least once a day, which was thoughtful. Mary would often complain to me that it was sometimes nearly six in the evening before she brought the paper in, and she would stay for a few minutes' chat, when Mary just wanted to get her dinner or watch the news on television, and she would have no time to do the crossword. How you have no time to do a crossword when you're retired I have never understood.

The trouble was that, as the twins had grown and I had gained more independence, so Mary's arthritis had become worse, and she was less able to get out and about. It's hard to say at what point exactly her interest became intrusive, but one day I realised that Mary was phoning me every single day, assuming I was available either to meet her or perhaps to take her out.

She had been very upset at giving up her driving licence. I had spent a whole morning working through the figures with her. If she put aside, perhaps in a separate Post Office account, the money she would otherwise have spent on fuel, tax, insurance and repairs, along with the capital sum that was yielded when she disposed of the car itself, this would then be a generous fund that she could use for taxis to go wherever and whenever she wanted. She wouldn't miss that money as she would have been spending it anyway. She was not entertaining that idea at all. She used a taxi once, to take her the doctor's surgery, where she asked the driver to wait for her, then take her on to the hospital, where again she kept him waiting. The cost was quite high by anyone's reckoning, and she refused to use taxis after that. Instead she would insist that she couldn't go anywhere unless she was taken, and every trip involved a moan about having been forced to give up her own car.

Cracks in our friendship, such as it was, deepened when my husband's job changed. I hadn't worked since the twins were born and then when our third baby came along things were pretty hectic and I had little time to think about myself never mind my neighbour, but Dave was offered a promotion, and so we had a house move to contend with as well. I have to accept that Mary was useful. She occasionally offered to have the children, always had the kettle on if I had to leave them with her for a short while, but it really didn't make her more likeable as a person.

The move took us a short distance away, to the

other side of town, and she could no longer see our front window from hers. The relief was immense on my part. It felt like I had escaped from some awful supervisor in a job I'd never applied for. A big advantage on the freedom front was that our new house, necessarily bigger because of our growing family, was at the top of a hill. We had decided that, with both of us having a car, and Dave's additional income, that would pose little problem. The downside from Mary's perspective was the distance. We now lived about a half hour drive away from our old home.

I gradually managed to wean Mary off our frequent visits, although not the invasive telephone calls. She would ring every day, without fail. If I did not answer, then she would try again later until I did. The conversations would often go something like this:

Mary: 'I rang you earlier.'
Me: 'Did you?'
Mary: 'Yes, where were you?'
Me: (Sometimes, when I'd had enough of being interrogated,) 'Out.'
Mary: 'There's no need to be like that.'
Me: 'I'm not being like anything, I had stuff to do, that's all. Not interesting stuff, just stuff.'

I was always left feeling guilty that I had not been prepared to be there at her beck and call, but Dave put his foot down, 'You mustn't let her guilt you into acting like her servant. Her situation is very unfortunate but it's not your fault and your first responsibility is to yourself and our family.'

After a while we settled into a routine. There was a particular charity Coffee Morning that she liked to go to every month but, for some reason, her next door neighbour would no longer be available to take her. My guess is that they too were feeling hard done by. I said that I could take her as I had done sometimes in the past, and it made me feel better. I suppose because selfishly it salved my conscience. This went on for several years. Although there were some hiccups, some expectations on her part that I felt were unreasonable.

For instance one morning when I called for her there was a strange car parked in her driveway. On the way to the Coffee Morning I asked her about it, and was told that her daughter and son-in-law had come to stay for the weekend. We parked in town quite near a local supermarket as usual, and on this occasion as I parked up, Mary said, 'I must remember to pop into the supermarket before we leave, I need some cat food.' No *Please;* no *If it's convenient;* or *If you can spare the time.*

Only we all know that in the middle of a Saturday morning, nobody just 'pops' into one of the big four supermarkets. It's a half hour job at the very least. I said nothing, hoping she would forget when it came time to leave the coffee morning, which she did.

When we got back to her house, her daughter and son in law were sitting relaxing in the sitting room, 'I didn't know May was coming to stay,' I said, 'Perhaps she would have enjoyed the Coffee Morning?'

'Oh, but they never get up till about ten o'clock. They like a lie in.' I was told.

Lucky them! Her daughter had the grace to blush. Perhaps she could see that I may have liked a lie-in as well, not that I ever got one with three small children. Admittedly it was a long journey they had made the night before, and it crossed my mind that both of Mary's children lived just about as far away as possible without emigrating. May and her family lived in the North East somewhere, and her brother had moved to Brighton.

Then one day Mary gave me a real fright. I had phoned earlier in the week as usual, to make sure she wanted to go to the Coffee Morning, it not being something I'd choose to go to on my own. It was a round trip of nearly thirty miles after all. She said it was on the calendar, and so I called round for her at nine thirty on the Saturday as usual. The door was locked, which was unknown. Generally she unlocked it when she first got up, so that I could get in, just in case she was finishing dressing, or doing her hair. I knocked and rang the bell over and over, but there was no reply. I walked across to the front corner of her bungalow. The lounge curtains were open, but there was nobody there. I passed her bedroom window, but the blinds were down so I couldn't see whether or not she was inside. By this time my mind was in overdrive. Entering the little road where we too had once lived, I had passed Mary's next door neighbours going out in their car and I knew of nobody else who might have a spare key to her house.

As I reached the corner of the property I noticed that the shower was running. Had Mary fallen? Was she struggling to get up? Was she running late and only just getting in the shower? I had no way of knowing. I was debating between whether to phone Dave, who had taken the children swimming and would not be pleased, and phoning the police. As I stood there the shower stopped flowing. So at least I knew that Mary had been able to turn it off. I hurried round to the front door again and rang and rang on the bell. Eventually Mary, wearing a bathrobe, hobbled through and unlocked it.

'What are you doing here?' were her opening words.

'It's Coffee Morning, I've come to collect you.'

'The Coffee Morning is next week, it's on my calendar.'

'I don't think so, Mary. It's today. We spoke about it on Tuesday, and it's always the second Saturday in the month, but we don't have to go if you don't have time to get dressed. We can perhaps just have a cup of tea here.'

That was too much to hope for. Mary told me she would just go and get dressed, and before I sat down to wait for her, I nipped into her kitchen to check her calendar on the wall. *Coffee Morning* was clearly marked next to that day's date.

From then I decided that I would gradually phase out the Coffee Mornings. I didn't want to be unkind to Mary, but that visit had really frightened me. If she had fallen, there's no way I could have picked her up, she's a big, heavy woman. I couldn't have even got to her without breaking in or calling the authorities.

I deliberately missed the following month and I lied about the reason. I'm not proud of that but I didn't want to hurt her feelings by telling her that I didn't want to, that these days she was too much of a responsibility and it was likely that, as time went on, she would become more so, so I made up an excuse that the children had a commitment. The truth was that I had just started working again now that the children were all at school, and the weekends were precious, and busy.

I couldn't do that to her on two consecutive months, and just before the next coffee morning she phoned me, 'I can't go on Saturday, but I've got some stuff you could take for me.'

How to respond? One of my issues was that, whether she was going or not, I ended up carrying whatever *stuff* she was donating across from the public car park to the village hall where the coffee morning and bric-a-brac sale was held. I didn't feel I had much choice; it took her all her time to stay upright across the cobbles, whether she used her stick or her walker. I preferred her taking the stick, because the walker isn't the easiest thing to get in and out of the car, and of course that job was left for me.

'I'd put it out in one of those charity bags, but they haven't taken it. I've no room for it lying around here.' She lived alone in a three-bedroomed bungalow with a garage and no car, so it seemed to me that one bag, even a big charity bag if it was full to overflowing, wasn't going to take up much room, but still.

'Mary, I won't be going without you. It's a long journey from here just to take your stuff.'

'Oh, I thought that as you wouldn't have anything else planned anyway ...' she sounded semi-hopeful.

There it is again, the guilt trip. I decided this had to be resolved once and for all. 'Mary, I go to the Coffee Morning to take you. If you don't go then I have other stuff to be doing.' It must have sounded harsh, or else she felt she'd been caught out, because she couldn't have sounded more hurt if I'd slapped her. Gradually things got back to normal for a few months, then Mary blew it totally.

Since the slip up with the shower, I had got into the routine of phoning her the day before Coffee Morning day. On this particular week, I phoned and she said she would love to go, and she said she had some stuff to go. My heart sank, but I was gradually managing to increase the gaps between these visits. Early on the Saturday morning, at about seven thirty, there was a phone call on our seldom-used landline. It says something for our relationship that over all the years I had known her, I had avoided ever giving Mary my mobile phone number. I looked at my husband, 'Perhaps she's changed her mind,' he said, but what she said floored me completely; the arrogance, the thoughtlessness I would have said was beyond even Mary.

'Hello,' she croaked down the phone, 'I won't be able to go today. I'm not too good.'

I asked her what was wrong.

'I tested positive for Covid yesterday morning. I felt okay, but I'm really rough this morning. I just can't face it.'

'Well thanks for letting me know now, and I hope you're soon on the mend, but are you saying that you knew yesterday that you had Covid, yet you said nothing about it when I phoned you. Why didn't you mention it then? I spoke to you yesterday evening to remind you about the Coffee Morning today!'

'Yes, but I was hoping I'd be all right, I felt reasonable yesterday. I could go but it's left me with no energy.'

I'm afraid I exploded, 'You just weren't going to say anything, were you? Until you decided that you couldn't face going out. You would have let me sit in an enclosed car with you; you would have gone round the bric-a-brac stalls, where there are a lot of people crushed together, a lot of older people, and children. You would have stood and breathed over the cake and plant stalls, and the counter where we grab a coffee, where there are plates of biscuits laid out? You would have done all that and said nothing?'

I was furious. She had known the previous day that she had tested positive for Covid and yet she was going to keep quiet. Just selfishly to go to an event that happens month in, month out. I was astounded at the arrogance and the selfishness. I was so angry. Then I told her that I wouldn't be going to the Coffee Mornings again; not taking her, and not taking her goods for the bric-a-brac stall. I was very sorry but she would have to make other arrangements.

I spoke to Dave and the children about it over lunch, and how I felt bad about it. One of my daughters was adamant that Mary wasn't my responsibility, and I suppose that's true. She does have her own family, but both live about as far away as they could. One of my three echoed my thought that there may be a reason for that. The twins both thought the same as Dave, that I was right to step away, but that her family should step up and take responsibility for Mary.

I disagreed. 'I would hate to think,' I told them, 'that you or your siblings helped us out when we are old, through a sense of obligation. If you really wanted to, then we could talk about it, but it's a Victorian concept, having children to look after one in one's dotage.'

'But your parents should be honoured, Mum,' one of the twins told me.

'And wouldn't that include honouring my decision that I refuse to be an imposition on the family when I'm old? I'm not saying that this is how Mary feels, I'm pretty sure she doesn't, she's been happy enough to impose herself on me and the neighbours, but it's certainly how I feel about you.

'If Mary wanted to, she can probably afford to move nearer one or other of her children; maybe not the son and his family in Brighton, but May lives in the North East. If they wanted to they could undoubtedly make better arrangements for her. All I can do is back off, and internally say: *Sorry Mary. It's Not My Problem.* I don't feel good about it though.'

Life blundered on, as it tends to do, for another eight months or so. I had heard nothing of Mary, then I had a phone call from her daughter, who had found my number in her mother's phone. She was calling to let me know the arrangements for her mother's funeral. Mary had died after suffering a stroke the previous Saturday night.

Just another few months of giving her one morning a month would have been all it took to keep her happy till she died. I felt really bad about her death. It was none of my doing, nothing to do with me really, but Guilt doesn't know that.

All Change at Number Twelve

It's a couple of years now since we moved house, and you need to know a little bit about our old property. The orientation of the house was unfortunate. Although detached, it had a whole wall that contained no windows whatsoever, neither upstairs nor down. This was because it directly abutted a narrow public footpath. Beyond this path was an old orchard that the owner was gradually converting to a garden. His family had owned their terraced property from new, and his grandfather had planted a row of eight sycamore trees just inside the boundary with the path. These were now mature trees, considerably taller than our house and these trees were protected with a preservation order.

I ask you! Sycamores, possibly the biggest weeds in the UK, and these were protected. They can undoubtedly be beautiful trees, but planted within a metre and a half of a dwelling, with the leaf fall in autumn, and the seeds falling all over our garden in spring, they were a nuisance.

The orientation of the house meant that there

was plenty of light throughout the day, but the back of the house, because of the trees, tended to be dark, in spite of a large kitchen window, and patio doors in the living room. When we showed Damien, the prospective purchaser, around he and his wife made no comment on the light factor and the sale went ahead. They were local people, familiar with the house before they bought it.

Then recently, quite by chance, I met Noel, our old next door neighbour in the supermarket; not the guy with the orchard, but from the detached house on the other side. He seemed incredibly pleased to see me, grinning like the proverbial Cheshire cat, but I was surprised when he invited me to join him for a cup of tea in the shop's café. 'I'm so glad I've met you,' he said, 'I don't suppose you've heard much about the family that has moved in to your old house?'

I might have refused but I was fascinated to hear about the young family who had bought number twelve. I had driven past the end of the cul de sac quite often, and they were clearly having extensive work done. I wondered what, and whether they had realised all of the rather grandiose changes they had talked about before we exchanged contracts.

Noel and I sat at one of the supermarket café tables, coffee and cake between us. After the usual generalities – how was his wife? How was my husband? Would they be going on holiday this year? we got down to the gossip.

He was smirking away and I asked him what was so funny. He told me that the people next door had commissioned a lot of alterations to be done, and he related a conversation he had with their builder one day when Damien and his family were not at home.

An enormous waggon had arrived that morning, stacked with seven or eight huge steel joists on the back. Noel said he couldn't resist asking the builder about them and where on earth they were for. The builder burst out laughing. He asked whether Noel knew how much Damien's family had paid for the house. When Noel told them what we had put it on the market for – it wasn't a secret, it was advertised in the local press and on line at the time – he laughed even more and said that Damien had now spent more than that on the changes he had wanted making, and they weren't finished yet!

Damien had told Noel not long after they moved in that his wife found the kitchen too dark. That was not surprising. Built onto the back of the kitchen, accessed via a utility room was a small glass clad sunroom. Except that the sun only reached that aspect for about half an hour each winter's day, and for the duration of the evening in the summer.

The couple had approached the paddock's owner about having the sycamore trees removed but he absolutely refused. He was very nostalgic about them as a link to his grandfather, and it had been when a previous owner of number twelve had approached with the same proposition before we moved in, that he had applied for, and been granted, the preservation order on them by the council.

Noel took one of the café's disposable napkins and mapped out roughly a floor plan of the external walls of number twelve. Then he drew in eight dotted lines before putting his pen down. I was puzzled, and he burst out laughing.

'That's it,' he said, 'they have moved the kitchen to what used to be the garage, and, except for the downstairs loo, they have taken down every single internal wall on the ground floor. The eight dotted lines are the RSJ's that were on that waggon, and they are all that is holding up the upstairs.' He sat back waiting for my reaction.

It seemed ridiculous, Damien had laid out considerably more than two hundred thousand pounds, just on alterations, none of which would solve the darkness issue that his wife had mentioned. In fact, in moving the kitchen into what had been the garage, the problem could be even worse. That would get the early morning sun, then nothing else all day.

They also had a growing family, who would not necessarily want to spend time with their parents in an open plan living room/kitchen/dining room, when their boyfriends and girlfriends came on the scene.

'What would you have done?' I asked Noel.

Always a bit of a rebel, he said: 'I'd have taken a chainsaw to the trees. Okay, I'd have ended up in court and with a huge fine, but surely not anything like he's paying out. With the cost of the house, and the changes so far, he's paid out over four hundred thousand, and at least the light issue would be solved.'

I drank up my coffee and left. Knowing Noel, I wouldn't put it past him, but I was left wondering why Damien and his family had bought number twelve in the first place, and just how long they would stay there.

Where has James Gone?

I'm a very worried dog this morning. I keep looking out of the front window but there's no sign of James anywhere, and I don't know where he's gone. I'm very concerned about him. We're not close friends, never have been. I can be a bit noisy and boisterous, and he's just a little boy, but it's reassuring that I see him pretty much every day, usually several times a day, especially first thing in the mornings, but not this week.

My human, Delphine, follows the same routine pretty much each day. I wake her some time after seven o'clock wanting breakfast and to go outside for a tinkle. While I'm doing that she'll make a piece of toast, and prime the coffee pot with her day's ration of caffeine. Then she opens the curtains, and we both snuggle up together on the comfy chair in the window. Generally Delphine will catch up on the day's news, or read her book, and I go back to sleep; but not until I've checked James is okay.

James lives across the road from us, not directly opposite, but a couple of houses further up the hill, and from the comfy chair I can see his bedroom window. Some time around eight o'clock his blind will open and there is James, bouncing on his bed and looking over at me. He gives me a wave, and sometimes draws patterns on the glass window. Often he plays with the blind, which I don't think is allowed, because if his mum or dad comes in he stops that straightaway. I'm not surprised they don't approve. Sometimes it seems he swings on it so hard it could come crashing down on his head.

That hasn't happened yet. And today I'm concerned because the blind was already open when I got up, and James isn't there, and neither are their two cars. I saw him yesterday. He and his mum and dad were in and out a lot and then a great big van arrived in the middle of the morning, and was parked outside their house for most of the day.

There are no lights on either, and yet it will soon be Christmas. This is especially worrying because a couple of weeks ago, like every other year, James's daddy put a string of fairy lights around their front door, and along the edge of the garage, and right out to the gate. His mummy put a Christmas tree up in the front window, and the lights flashed on and off every day, from the time James was due home from school, until his mummy and daddy went to bed.

Then, four days ago, the lights were not lit anymore. I wondered if they had broken, but it seemed a bit odd for the outside lights and the inside lights on the tree to have broken at the same time. On my morning walk I looked especially, and the lights had been taken down and so had the tree! And still there was no sign of James.

Delphine has put our Christmas tree up in the front window and it's blocking my view a little. Still, I would see the movement if James was in his room, he's like a bouncing ball, never still. He and I came to live with our families at about the same time although I think via different routes. I'm not sure but I think they grew James themselves, whereas I was chosen from a rescue shelter. I guess that makes me special doesn't it, but it certainly helped us to be friends. He would jump on the bed, which I'm not allowed to do sadly as it looks fun. Sometimes he would pull so hard on the cord attached to the blind that it would fly up really quickly and he would laugh and try to do it again. One time he had opened the window and was leaning out. Nobody seemed to notice and I was frightened that he'd fall, then suddenly his daddy appeared in the window beside him, shouting so loudly that I could hear him here across the road. I think he was only shouting because he was frightened for James too, and James had a little cry, then they cuddled for a while and James never did it again.

It's the fifth day now, and still I don't know what's happened. It's like a ghost town over there and I can't figure out why. The only other strange thing I can remember is that huge blue van turning up over there one morning, blocking out my view of their house completely for almost the whole day. After that their cars were gone and that's the last we saw of them. Until this evening.

Delphine answered the door and James and his mummy were standing there with a bag of parcels. 'This is presents for you,' James said, and pushed the bag into the hall.

His mummy explained, 'You have been such lovely neighbours, I wanted to thank you for everything you've done for us.' Delphine said that we hadn't done anything really, but it was very nice of them, and then I understood.

'How did the move go? It's stressful isn't it?'

'It went as well as it could. James stayed a couple of nights with his grandma,' Ah – so that's one mystery solved, 'it all happened really quickly in the end. The people coming into our old house have no chain, and will be moving in tomorrow I think. I'm not sure of their circumstances, but at least we didn't have to get out in time for them to move in on the same day. It meant we could be a bit more relaxed.'

'I've got a new bedroom,' James told me, while the adults were talking, 'and it's going to have rockets on the wallpaper after Christmas. Daddy put the Christmas lights up at the new house yesterday, and the tree.'

'The people who are moving in, have a couple of children and a young puppy, so they have their hands full,' James's mummy said.

Delphine waved them off after I had given James a goodbye lick. Two children and a puppy! That could be fun. I might have to help the puppy learn about the traffic and things, and it sounds as if the two children are company for each other. I always felt a bit sorry for James, as he was an only one and most of the people round here are much older grown-ups. There are no small children at all. His mummy said that they have moved much nearer to James's school and to where most of his friends live, so that will be better for him.

I can't wait now for tomorrow. I expect there will be another van blocking my view all day, but once it's gone it will be fun to look out for children, and a puppy, about the place again.

Otto

Otto was brought to the UK from Germany when Albert returned after the Great War in 1919. Albert had a young daughter whom he had never seen although Kitty was then nearly five years old. Like all those who are involved in terrible atrocities, the Albert who returned was a very different person from the eager young man who had enlisted for the army in 1914.

Otto was unpacked and placed at the centre of the marital bed. His wife at first thought that Albert had managed to get a birthday present for Kitty, but the doll was tattered and stained. She stood holding it wondering, when Albert came and screamed at her to put Otto down, never to touch Otto again, and not to let her daughter near him. That was how he referred to Kitty – *your daughter*. He spent the rest of the day cradling Otto in his arms like a fetish, crooning to him as Kitty cowered in the kitchen and her mother painted on a brave smile. This was not the homecoming that they had so keenly anticipated since the Armistice.

Gradually Albert shared some of Otto's story

with his wife. He had taken the doll from the hands of a little girl of about Kitty's age. Or rather from the hand as that was all that he could see of her projecting from underneath the rubble caused by his battalion's advance one morning. As he moved the doll the little girl's hand came away from her arm. He still suffered nightmares about that girl recovering and chasing him, resulting often in him waking screaming in the night with the neighbours banging on the walls.

Kitty and Albert were strangers and the little girl was terrified. She had often been told that her Daddy would be coming home and they would be a proper family, perhaps that there would be a little brother or sister for her. But Albert shunned physical contact of all kinds, and would only briefly tolerate being held at the height of his night terrors, until he recovered enough to grab Otto and move away from his wife.

'Is the dolly for me?' Kitty asked him on the morning of her birthday.

'He's not a dolly, he's Otto. He's not to be played with by a child. Of course he's not for you.' And Albert took up his regular crooning and rocking pose by the fire, explaining to Otto that they were all stupid people, to be ignored and that he would look after Otto properly. Eyeing him carefully, Kitty opened the colouring book and crayons her mother had been able to secure as a present.

It was recognised that the stresses of war could cause men to break down, but at that time there was a general belief that a lasting episode was symptomatic of an underlying lack of character. A real man would pull himself together and get over it. Life struggled along for the family. Albert was unable to find work;

there was so much competition from other returning servicemen who were diligent and hardworking, whereas he was flighty, inclined to explode at the slightest criticism. Several times he secured a job, only to walk away from it after a day or so, unable to cope. The cleaning and sewing that his wife did around the town, barely brought in enough money to support them, although the women in general were sympathetic and tried to put work her way. It was clear to those who knew him that Albert's health had suffered terribly through his ordeals during the conflict, and after a couple of years he was admitted to hospital, taking Otto with him.

Albert lived on in the hospital until his death in 1922. Amongst the possessions returned to the family was his doll Otto. Thinking back to how Albert had been when they first met and married, his wife kept Otto as a memento in her bedroom, where he sat on the window ledge, facing outwards.

That is, sometimes he faced outwards, but she swore that sometimes, on opening the curtains, Otto was in a different position, facing where her head had been resting on the pillow. She told her daughter that she was now allowed to play with Otto, but Kitty was not to be won over. She determinedly avoided entering a room where she knew Otto was, but nevertheless several times came across him; once he was on the living room sofa, where neither she nor her mother admitted to putting him. A friend had been to play and was presumed to be the culprit.

Kitty had asked her mother to throw Otto away, but strangely Albert's widow was becoming more attached to the odd little doll. It became like a talisman; a memorial to her late husband. She said that

Otto reminded her of Albert as he used to be in happier times before the outbreak of war.

One afternoon Albert's widow found herself pitying Otto his dirty, torn state. She took out her sewing box and made him an outfit of trousers and jacket out of Albert's old clothes. She tried not to think about the stains she was covering, maybe blood from the little German girl who had owned him, or dirt from the battle site. She sponged his fabric gently, cradling him like a baby, yet the stains remained, testimony to his past.

His face was not attractive. Either through the love of the little girl or the hatred of war, his nose was rubbed away almost to nothing, just two unsightly pinholes. One side of his mouth had come unstitched and Kitty's mother carefully threaded the loose strand of silk into her needle and tacked it back down. It wasn't a smile on Otto's face, more a leer, but his mouth was secure and would not unravel further. One of his button eyes had been wrenched from his head and this presented more of a problem. There was a gaping hole where the eye should be and a neat darn was needed to close it. She recognised that it would be a weak area and so Otto's new eye was attached several millimetres higher up his face. Kitty's mother laughed and crooned quietly as she worked.

'You look very handsome from this side Otto, almost like you're winking at me. From the other side though, not so good – you look quite sinister, it's a pity I can't do anything about your nose, or the stains ingrained in your body. Never mind, you look much better than you did, especially with these new clothes.' Kitty, coming in from school and eavesdropping outside the door, heard the last couple of words and wondered which of her mother's dressmaking customers was being spoken to; probably one of the ladies from the town. She knocked and entered, surprised to find her mother sitting with Otto on her knee, as she had often seen her father, and there was no-one else in the room.

Only by placing the doll outside the house could Kitty be enticed in to eat, but after she was asleep her mother retrieved the doll and replaced him in her own bedroom. As she sat him down, she was sure that he was smiling at her. Ridiculous – it was just the new stitching to his face, wasn't it? She shivered.

That night Kitty heard a conversation, seeming to come from the loft. Her mother, and a young boy. Was it Otto? It couldn't be and yet . . . there seemed to be a faintly German accent. She crept up the stairs and listened as her mother talked to the doll in a lilting, crooning voice. Surprisingly the doll, seemingly talked back to her. Often, on Kitty's return from school, she would find the two like this, almost as if Otto had taken over Albert's place in her mother's life. Before long she began to consult the doll before taking any decisions, however minor, and the downhill slide in her mental health seemed to accelerate.

One day in 1928, just after Kitty had arrived home from the shop where she worked, laden with shopping for her mother no longer ventured outside, she found her mother on the floor alongside Otto. She was still alive, but unable to speak or move and she lived on for only another couple of days.

At her mother's funeral Kitty didn't know what to do with the doll, it had seemed such an integral part of her parents' lives, and her own since she was five years old. She thought about placing Otto in her mother's coffin, but then placed him on the kitchen windowsill, where he was the first thing she saw on coming down each morning. It was strange living in an otherwise empty house. She could almost see the attraction of talking to an inanimate object such as Otto, especially as these days his face seemed less sinister, and there was almost a crooked smile that made her inclined to smile in return. She found also that although she never discussed the doll with anybody else, to herself she had stopped thinking about *it*, and instead thought of the doll as *him*.

She gave herself a good talking to. She would throw Otto away. The bin would be emptied and she would forget all about the creepy little doll that seemed to have dominated most of her childhood.

She got as far as opening the door to take him out to the bin, but from the corner of her eye she was sure that she saw Otto move, and she hurriedly closed it again. He had definitely changed position. His lip curled sneeringly and one eye winked.

Kitty ran terrified into the kitchen, grabbed a breadknife and was found ten minutes later screaming and stabbing and stabbing at the doll on the kitchen table in a fit of hysteria. The neighbour who found her led her into the living room and called the authorities. Kitty vaguely heard him describing the incidence of mental health issues evidenced in both of her parents.

When Kitty had been taken from the house, the neighbour went back to the bin. As they drove Kitty away, he retrieved the little brown doll, ugly and a bit grubby, but maybe it would clean up. He was sure his young daughter would love to play with it.

Fortunately Kitty's stabbing had missed the doll completely and it was totally intact. She had simply gouged again and again at the wooden kitchen table.

As he picked it up, he wondered what it was that had tipped Kitty over the edge like that; certainly not this cute little doll. He took it next door and showed it to his wife, along with the story of Kitty's crisis. His wife declared that she would clean it up and make it new clothes, perhaps something prettier. She laid it beside her on the chair, failing to see the mouth curl to the side in a sneer, and the one remaining eye open and stare at her.

Unlucky for Some

His mother stuck her head around the kitchen door just as he was about to leave the house, 'Freddy, if you're going into town, take Gran's library books will you, and pick her another couple please.'

Gran, his grandmother, had lived with Freddy's family as long as he could remember, and really impacted very little on Freddy's life. Perhaps if he returned her books first, then left choosing new ones till later, he needn't have the books with him when he met his friends. He didn't want them poking fun at the twee titles and pink book covers she favoured.

She'd always been a prolific reader, getting through at least a couple of books a week. Even when he was small he knew that after he had gone to bed each night Gran went and had a long, lazy bath. She said it eased her aching back and hips. He would often get up in the morning to use the bathroom and find a book, opened out and pages down, stretched across the bathroom radiator. In his young head he had come up with an explanation of his own. He decided that it was expected, before returning a borrowed library book, that you washed and dried it.

He believed that for some time, until his mother caught him washing a book, and explaining what damage that would do. She laughed at his idea that this was what Gran did with library books, and explained that often Gran just fell asleep in the warm water, the book slipped out of her hands and had to be dried before she could continue to read it.

He wasn't exactly ashamed of the old woman, but the books that she read were weird. They all had titles like the two he would be returning today, *Nurse Nancy's Wild Streak,* and *The Winter Warmers at Number Sixteen.* He guessed that there would be plenty of innuendo for his friends to find if they saw him with these.

The library was warm but instead of the pretty young librarian with the warm smile at the counter, it was the one who was much older. She wore stout shoes and a grey cardigan and looked very scholarly. She opened the books and took out his Gran's tickets, but instead of handing them to him, she fixed Freddy with a gimlet gaze.

'We come across a lot of people who deface library books, young man. Very often we can't catch them, but in this case – she slapped her hand down on the two volumes – because *Nurse Nancy's Wild Streak* is a brand new book and Mrs Dylan was the first person to borrow it, we know that the damage has been done whilst it was in her keeping, and that it has been done deliberately.

She indicated the little line drawn across the corner of page 13; the indication for whoever chose new books for Gran, that she had already read this one. On this occasion Gran had used biro to draw the line, and been particularly heavy-handed. Freddy felt himself blush.

'Please, it's nothing to do ...' but of course it had something to do with him, which is what he had been about to deny. 'It's just so that we don't get her a book she's already had.'

She drew herself up to her full height, and boomed at him, much to his embarrassment, 'Oh, I know what it's for, young man. Hundreds of people use our lending library. How do you think it would be if everyone who borrowed books did something similar? Would you find that acceptable?'

Freddy didn't use the library much and didn't really mind one way or the other, but that clearly wasn't the right answer here, 'No, I'm sorry,' he blustered, 'I'll tell her not to do it again.'

'No! I'll tell her not to do it again,' boomed the woman, who seemed to be growing in stature all the time. She drew a printed form out of her draw, and filled in some of the blank spaces on it, Gran's name and address, library registration number and Freddy's full name. She then insisted that he sign the form. He had a quick look down it; it was all about promises not to deface public property, and what penalties could be applied if it happened again.

The librarian was still speaking, 'Now I know the mark Mrs Dylan has used I will be looking out for them, and there will be penalties. You can tell Mrs Dylan that. I've put it in the letter. Now, can I trust you to pass this letter on to her or had I better post it?'

'I'd rather you posted it please,' Freddy flushed bright red, 'you see, if I take the letter it's bound to be my fault somehow.'

The librarian faltered, 'I don't think it is your fault, not initially, so what I will do is alter this letter slightly and I'll tuck the form with your signature out of the way here in my drawer. We have to stop this sort of thing so I can't just ignore it, but I can make it perhaps seem that we were doing random checks and that is how we found it.

'That would keep you personally out of it. It wouldn't be fair if you got into trouble when this has obviously been going on for a long time. I suspect your mum and your gran have been doing it for years haven't they?'

Freddy nodded, 'I think so. This is the first time I've brought the books back and was just told what to look out for.'

Under the librarian's watchful gaze, he grabbed two different books for Gran, and slunk up to the desk. There was no way he felt up to meeting his friends this afternoon.

Freddy scuttled out of the library as quickly as he could. He would make an excuse for not meeting his friends, instead he would just walk home. It would help him to calm down, but he wouldn't be getting any more library books for Gran. He wasn't going through that again. Page 13 and their secret code was not of interest to him any longer, it was unlucky for Freddy and he would have nothing more to do with it.

Green Beans and Baby Carrots

'Do you need any help, Ma?' he called, already knowing what the reply would be. He parodied along with her voice from the kitchen, *'No thanks, dear. You just read the paper. Tea won't be long.'*

Tea! It was dinner that he and Tara ate at this time of day, and he had called it that for years, but he'd never change his mother's ways now. She was too old, too stuck in the past. His mother had served tea when his Dad came home from work, and now she would do the same for her son when he came to visit.

'Would you like me to set the table?'

'No love, you just sit there. I'll do it; while the veg is cooking.' She went to the sideboard, and got out mats, paper serviettes and the best cutlery, slowly setting the table in the little-used dining room. The room would have been cleaned within an inch of its life that morning and a strong smell of lavender furniture polish permeated every meal he ate there.

Gideon allowed his thoughts to drift back to the cottage, and to what he and Tara could be having for their evening meal. There were two lovely salmon steaks ready to poach and serve with maybe a baked potato and some cheese sauce from the freezer. Or there was broccoli and stilton soup and some lovely crunchy garlic bread that could be followed by a light dessert, a sorbet perhaps or a few grapes with cheese.

Here, at his mother's, the joint would be beef, or chicken, or maybe pork; although no, she didn't really trust pork, not unless it was cooked for a day and half *just in case*. Beef was fairly expensive and the price of lamb was astronomical, so his guess was chicken.

'It's chicken, is that okay, Gideon?' the voice of doom from the kitchen.

'Lovely, Ma. Thanks.' There was no question that there would be potatoes, boiled to death in water with far too much salt for his taste. His ma persisted in thinking that eating healthily meant eating as much as possible. There would be the inevitable soggy boiled potatoes paddling in an enormous lake of gravy the consistency of warm tap water.

And here we have it, the crowning glory: green beans and baby carrots, not gently steamed or delicately glazed in honey, but boiled. And boiled, and then boiled some more.

'Would you like salt?' Ma asked when they were seated, pushing the condiment towards him, but he was too quick for her, 'No, I'll taste it first Ma, thanks. We don't tend to use much salt these days.' He tried to find a positive, 'the chicken smells delicious.'

She beamed, that once again she had delighted her only son.

And now came Gideon's dilemma, how to eat this abomination before him. It was served, as always, on a cold plate, and already the watery gravy was beginning to congeal in unappealing greasy blobs around the edge. The ambient temperature would advise eating it quickly before it was all cold, but this may give too much of an impression of enjoyment and the empty plate would quickly be replenished with admonishments about him not eating enough to keep a fly alive.

He toyed with the idea of excusing himself from the table for a few minutes so that he could pop the plate in the microwave before he retook his seat. He might even be able to sneak some of it into the bin under the sink. But no, it would be noticed next time Ma came to throw something away. It would be too cruel after she had worked to put the meal together for him. He would just have to plough on; not too quickly, not too slowly.

'More vegetables, Gideon? There are plenty.' Ma hopefully lifted a serving spoonful, and he wondered idly what she did with all the leftovers, of which there must be lots as they went through this farce every time he visited. His thoughts were momentarily distracted by thoughts of the fresh half head of cauliflower in the fridge at home. It would have been delicious served al dente with the salmon and cheese sauce he had been dreaming of earlier.

'Love?' His thoughts were interrupted, 'More veg?'

'Oh, no thanks Ma. I have plenty.' He was vaguely hoping that by spreading his leavings around the plate, they would appear less.

Eventually Ma sat back in her chair, declaring

herself full, and Gideon felt able to put down his knife and fork, trying not to belch.

'Ooh, I enjoyed that,' she said, 'I only ever get a roast on the days when you come up. It's not worth cooking a roast dinner just for myself. Now roly-poly pudding and custard for afters, your favourite.' She gathered the plates and headed to the kitchen.

My favourite when I was eight years old perhaps, Gideon thought, and only ever eaten at Ma's in the years since then. He looked at the bowl she placed in front of him, lukewarm pudding swimming in lumpy custard, and suddenly he had a plan, 'Tell you what Ma, next time why don't we go out to the pub when I come over; my treat?' He might have guessed the reaction before he'd finished the sentence.

'Oh, I don't think so, Gideon love, I don't like all that fancy food especially these days. It plays havoc with my digestion. Good plain, well-cooked British food is always best I think. I'll get a nice bit of pork in next time shall I? You don't need to worry, I'll make sure that it's thoroughly cooked.'

'That would be wonderful,' Gideon said, swallowing another belch and resolving to call at the late night pharmacy on his way home to buy a packet of Rennies.

Agony or Ecstasy

There's a very popular high street shop which sell lots of highly scented items, such as soap and shower gels, as well as that modern phenomenon, the bath bomb. The headquarters is based in Poole in Dorset, a town we often visited whilst holidaying. The offices were upstairs above a retail shop in the high street.

I should have seen it coming of course. He was a beagle, a scent hound, with however many more hundreds of scent receptors in his nose than a human has, and the place could be sniffed out halfway down the road. To be fair, my eyes started to water before we even got inside the shop, just walking past it was enough. There was a young lady assistant with green hair smoking on the doorstep.

'Oh, what a lovely doggy! Is it a he or a she? What's his name? Ah, lovely little man. He's a bit like Detective Columbo's dog isn't he?' All the usual things dog-owners are used to hearing from other dog-lovers.

I handed the lead to my husband, 'Hang on to

him will you? I want to get something to take back for our daughters. I won't be long.'

'Oh! You don't have to wait out here with him, he can come in the shop, bring him in.' There was a brief pause, 'he's not likely to lift his leg is he?'

My husband reassured her. We had struggled this holiday. Benji didn't like to lift his leg anywhere except on the potted plants in our garden. This proved quite a challenge when we were on holiday for a week in Dorset, but at least we could be sure that he wouldn't disgrace us in this or any other shop.

What we hadn't reckoned on though was the overpowering scent of candles, soaps, bath bombs, creams, facial scrubs, everything apparently essential to looking and smelling feminine. My husband, whose sense of smell is not good, was oblivious to the effect on the dog, walking around the shop slowly, picking up products and sniffing them.

It was as I moved round the back of a display unit of bath bombs, and met the two of them coming the other way that I spotted Benji's eyes. They were glazed over and rolling back in his head. The expression on his face was one I had never seen before, almost catatonic. He was taking in enormous sniffs of air, almost as if inhaling a drug of some sort, which in a way I suppose he was.

'Take him outside, quickly,' I hissed to my husband.

'What? Why?'

'Just do it, I'll join you in a minute.' Thankfully he took Benji out onto the footpath without any more questions. I made my purchases and joined them.

'What was all that about?' he asked as we

walked up the road into town.

I told him about the dog's expression, the eyes almost rolled back and glazed over; the apparent effort to take a normal breath, instead gasping these strange inhalations that I had never ever seen him do before.

'Did he like it in there, do you think?' he asked as we walked side by side, the dog now apparently back to normal.

'I can't say,' I told him, 'but he either thought it was heavenly, or he was about to pass out, and I'm not sure which.'

'Wow,' he said, 'Heaven or Hell, Agony or Ecstasy. Poor Benji, I guess we'll never know.'

Three Strikes and You're Out

Bunty had certainly proved satisfactory as a domestic cleaner and Diane had been congratulated by one of the mums at the school gate, in being lucky enough to employ her.

'She's particular,' she had been told, 'and I believe,' conspiratorially, 'that she even does ironing.'

Another advantage was that Diane's house could be seen, albeit some distance away, from the end of Bunty's road so she was local.

Nevertheless, paragon or not, there was something about Bunty that Diane didn't take to. She herself was out at work most of the time, so didn't have much to do with the cleaning lady, but something about her attitude rubbed Diane up the wrong way. She was glad that Bunty liked to start early in the day. That way Diane could let her in before she went to work. She would have felt uncomfortable entrusting Bunty with a key. It was gratifying, she had to admit, to come home once a week to a vacuumed house, bed linen changed, washed and in the tumble dryer, and a clutch of ironed shirts hanging over the rail.

One morning Diane had let Bunty in and left for work as usual. Before she even reached the motorway, a matter of a few miles away, her phone rang. It was today's client cancelling their meeting, as the person she was due to meet had called in sick. Diane sat for a few minutes in a layby, shuffling appointments in her diary, but there was nothing to do for the rest of this day other than to go home and catch up with some work there. She had a home office and could shut herself out of Bunty's way.

As she pulled into the drive she supposed that Bunty would hear her arrival. But she may not have done, as the television was blaring in the living room, and the radio blaring upstairs in the bedroom. In spite of this cacophony Bunty didn't appear to be slacking. She met Diane at the door, polish in one hand and a duster in the other. Diane wondered later whether Bunty had perhaps grabbed these as she heard the car arrive.

'Oh, you startled me,' she said, 'I wasn't expecting you.' She dashed to the television and turned it off. She slunk off upstairs, and turned off the radio. It was obvious that of course she hadn't expected Diane back. Strike number one!

Diane made allowances, it didn't really matter and she knew there were people who worked better with ambient noise. She stopped work at eleven and made them both a cup of coffee. Bunty stood at the kitchen window looking out at the garden.

'Your garden's looking lovely. My Maurice would love to have a look at it. He loves gardening you know.'

Diane was very proud of the view from her

windows, it was a big garden and she had spent the two years since they moved to the house, licking it into shape.

She was aware that Maurice worked shifts so she made a vague offer, 'Well, whenever he's available and I'm around, you're very welcome to bring him over. I'd be happy to show him, show you both, what we've done out there. You can see from the end of your road whether my car's here, so you won't have a wasted journey.'

A few weeks passed and the garden was not mentioned, until one day when Diane bumped into Bunty and Maurice at the supermarket. She restated the offer for Maurice to come and have a guided tour of the garden. Then she caught sight of the fury on Bunty's face. Maurice was no dissembler and he said quite blithely, 'Oh, we came round last Wednesday. Bunty was able to tell me about all the work you've done out, it looks really lovely out there.'

'Oh, I rather thought you'd come around while I was at home. As I suggested, Bunty.' Diane glared pointedly at her cleaner, who blushed, but more with anger at being put in the wrong, than with apology, and nothing more was said. Diane wondered whether the poor man would get a tongue-lashing once they had walked away. Strike number two!

As soon as she got home Diane phoned a local building firm she had used in the past. Within three weeks a fence and locked gate had been fitted between the garage and the corner of the house. She arranged also for security cameras to be set up. The encounter had been unsettling.

It was three weeks later that Diane let Bunty into the house as usual. She wasted no time in coming to the point.

'Bunty, I shan't be needing your services after today.'

'Oh, what?' Bunty was livid, 'Just like that? No notice? After all I've done for you. Well I've cleaned for better people than you, Madam so you can stick your job,' she started to zip up her coat, but Diane was between her and the door.

'Not so fast Bunty. There is one other thing you are going to do for me.'

'Nothing. No. I will not do anything at all for you . . .'

'Oh but you will, if you don't want me to involve the police.'

That shut her up. Then she said warily, 'What do you mean? Why would you involve the police?' Diane could see from Bunty's eyes that she knew exactly what was coming.

'The necklace, the one with an embroidered forget-me-not in the centre of it, that my mother gave to me, I want it back and I want it back today. I was looking in my jewellery box on Monday for something else. I spotted the necklace and decided to wear it tonight. When I came to get it out of the box just now, it had gone.'

'I don't know anything ... I haven't . . .'

Diane continued as if Bunty hadn't spoken, 'You are the only person who has been in here since Monday. You are the only person who could have taken it when you were here on Tuesday morning. And,' Diane flicked open her phone and scrolled down, 'This photograph of you taken in the Working Men's Club bar on Tuesday evening and posted onto social media by one of your friends, how do you explain the fact that you are wearing my necklace then?

'You know that we now have security cameras here. I shall be keeping a screenshot of this post and if I ever see you or Maurice on our property again I will be phoning the police. You will return that necklace by eight o'clock tonight or I shall be phoning the police about that anyway. I have been lenient with you. You had a cushy little job here Bunty, TV and radio blaring which I overlooked: then assuming that my invitation to Maurice was just permission to wander round my empty property whenever you wanted, in spite of me specifically mentioning that you were welcome to invite him when my car was here and I was therefore at home. I overlooked that as well, but not this. This is the end.

Three strikes and you're out.

An Advisory Tale

It started as a regular day, just like any other. The only thing in the diary was that the routine prescription needed collecting from the pharmacy. A ten minute walk to the village and back, half an hour in total. While she was there, Linda planned to buy wrapping paper, and a birthday card. She waved goodbye and set out on an adventure she certainly hadn't been expecting.

The pharmacy had recently changed their procedures. Instead of having prescriptions already made up, some of which were never collected, they would make them up when individuals arrived to collect them. So as soon as Linda arrived her prescription was passed to the pharmacist, who would make it up as soon as he was available.

'While you're waiting,' the assistant said, 'how about we take your blood pressure? It won't take long, and you're hanging around anyway.'

Linda had been about to go to the card shop, but that was no rush. At least agreeing to have her BP taken, she could sit down for a few minutes.

She was not someone who monitored her BP at all. With a slight tendency to hypochondria, she found that reading the possible side-effects on medication information was a sure fire way of experiencing such symptoms. So she had no idea what her BP readings should be.

The assistant placed the cuff on her left arm, and carried through the procedure, saying nothing. She then suggested they try the right arm. Job done, Linda asked, 'What does it read?'

'It's the systolic pressure that's most important here,' the assistant was beginning to look unsettled, 'It reads 180.'

'What should it be?'

'Ideally below 150. I'm just going to have a word with the pharmacist. Make sure the cuff's working properly.'

Enter the pharmacist, who repeated the process. The systolic reading, he told her was now 185. He filled figures in on his form and said that Linda was to go straight across the road to the GP surgery.

'But I don't have an appointment.'

'Don't worry about that. They will see you once they have a look at these numbers.'

Armed with the prescription that started it all, and with the printout she went to the GP's Reception, apologised that she had no appointment and explained what had happened. As soon as the Triage nurse was available she called Linda through. She again took the BP, twice, and disappeared with all the paperwork to show it to the GP. Linda never got to see the GP at all. The nurse simply came back with a message. 'You are to go straight to Accident and Emergency. Can you get there yourself or shall I call an ambulance?'

Regular phone conversations keeping her other half apprised of the situation led to him coming to collect her and taking her to the hospital. Immediately on handing over the documentation, another triage nurse took her BP again, the result of which readings leading to his suggestion that she be bumped up to the top of the list to see the doctor on duty, and so she had barely taken a seat in the waiting room before being called through.

Surprise, surprise, he took her blood pressure yet again. 'The systolic reading is 216,' he told her. 'I'm not surprised' she said, 'what happens now?'

'216 is a dangerously high reading. We recommend an immediate intervention at anything over 180, and hopefully we can get you down to 150.'

Dangerously high! He gave her a dose of medication, which he said needed an hour to act. If at that next reading the BP was down to 180or less she would be allowed to go home. Otherwise she would be given a further dose of medication, and she would then have to wait another hour. This first hour wouldn't be wasted, they would carry out blood and urine tests, take a heart X-ray and an ECG.

By the time that was done the hour was up. BP taken yet again, (it was taken twelve times in total that day), the reading was down to just above 180. The tests and X-ray were all clear and Linda was free to go home, via the hospital pharmacy.

Now settled on a regime of suitable medication, the difference in how she felt before this intervention, and since, is quite noticeable.

There's a moral to this tale. If you are offered a check of this sort, take the opportunity. Linda had noticed no symptoms whatever, which she learned is quite frequent in post-menopausal women particularly. Also on getting older, it's accepted that we're not in the *Turning Cartwheels* phase of our lives, and it's easy to write off any lack of energy as being natural.

A ten minute walk to the village for a bit of shopping had turned into a whole day out, but one that was very worthwhile.

The Book List

It was a great opportunity. Bonnie's husband had the offer of a short-term contract working in the United States, and Bonnie was hoping to spend some time there supporting children who struggled to learn reading, or perhaps had little access to books at home. The mismatch between holiday dates in the USA and at home meant that she would need very little time off her job as a teaching assistant, and the head teacher had been enthusiastic, seeing it as an opportunity to perhaps import different methods and ideas.

Bonnie had offered her services to the Governors of a local school, who had been very grateful to accept her offer of help, and had sent her the necessary insurance paperwork, and other documentation that had to be completed. She looked forward to introducing new readers to some of the children's books she shared with her little charges at home in the UK. It would be lovely to think that she could perhaps change the lives, to some small degree, of children on the other side of the Atlantic.

The reality was very different from Bonnie's

expectations. She had no children of her own, but a vast experience of working with all ages of infant and junior school youngsters. She was to be based in a small school in Dallas, Texas, and Bonnie had never come across anything like it. The USA, she had been led to believe, was the Land of the Free and Home of the Brave. But this visit to Texas was showing that, in some aspects at least, US citizens were far from free in the choices that they were allowed. The one that specifically impinged on Bonnie's plans was the list of restrictions on certain children's books.

What she had not expected was the involvement of the American Library Association, which was much more active in red states such as Texas, where she would be staying. It has a designated Banned Books Week each year, when so called subversive or unsuitable books are listed for the guidance of parents. This list encompasses a register of books that have been banned in schools and libraries by the authorities, and those which have received the most challenges from parents or other adults about their suitability as books for children. Some of these went on to be banned; others remained as *'Challenged'*. The list of these books, quite a hefty document, was not included with the paperwork she had received in the UK.

Bonnie had done a lot of her planning already before leaving the UK, with key texts already identified before she arrived, and these bans were to have a significant impact on those plans once she reached Texas. She checked the copy of the most recent Banned Books List and found, from talking to local parents, that there were still concerns on their part about books that had been banned or challenged, perhaps just for a short time and some of them many years previously. It seemed that few had issues about the authorities censoring what their children could or could not read. The attitude seemed to be that the 'professionals' had more right than parents to identify what was or was not suitable.

She read through the list in amazement. She didn't believe in banning books at all; was happy for children in her care to tackle reading pretty much anything, as long as there was an adult who could appropriately interpret, explain, discuss or criticise the text.

This list of books was, to her mind, horrific. One book was *The Wizard of Oz*. Bonnie remembered reading it as an early teen, and watching the film soon afterwards. The reasons listed for its ban were: 'Strong female characters; the use of magic; the promotion of socialist values, and attributing human characteristics to animals.'

Bonnie found herself laughing out loud, surely this was rubbish. She continued reading and the next novel to catch her eye was George Orwell's *1984*, a frequent text on the UK GCSE syllabus for sixteen-year-olds. This was identified as 'The Most Banned and Challenged Book in Texas of the past eight years'! This was for its 'Social and Political Themes, and for the promotion of socialism.' She could to some extent understand concerns about the text, but surely, delivered correctly, there was great scope for questioning and learning.

Here was another favourite; *Charlotte's Web,* which E.B.White wrote for children aged seven years and older, was banned for covering 'Death', and, like The Wizard of Oz, 'the main characters being talking animals.' This seemed to be something that really worried some American scholars, this time particularly in Kansas, another red state. There was a pattern emerging here.

The Lord of the Flies, another UK GCSE common text was perhaps more understandable. It has often been banned and is the eighth most frequently banned book from US schools as well as often being challenged. 'Violence, bullying and statements defamatory to God,' are the reasons cited in Iowa. Yet surely, Bonnie thought, that was the whole point. The books were written to be read with an adult's support if necessary, to affirm, dismiss or help formulate ideas. How could youngsters judge it if it was kept from them? Bonnie suspected that, in time, these books became under-the-counter transactions, with children backing them in brown paper to conceal what they really were. Rather like Lady Chatterley's Lover had been in the UK, although that was sixty five years ago, and the banning of it was swiftly overturned by a court case. Surely these bans would just reinforce that it was acceptable to be sneaky?

A lesser known book in the UK for eight to twelve year olds: *Harriet the Spy* by Louise Fitz was banned because 'it teaches lying, answering back, spying and' horror of horrors, 'cursing!'

She read on. *The Lion, the Witch and the Wardrobe* was not banned, but was challenged because of 'graphic violence, mysticism and gore', none of which she really recognised from her own reading of it, except perhaps mysticism. Given that this was part of the Narnia series, an explicitly Christian allegory written by the deeply religious C.S.Lewis it seemed, to Bonnie, all the more bizarre.

Thinking about witches, Bonnie cast her eye down the rest of the list where *The Witches* by Roald Dahl had caught her eye. Probably she shouldn't be surprised that this was included, given the Narnia posting, but again she was shocked that it was supposed to be written for eight to twelve year olds, yet was deemed to be 'too sophisticated, and not teaching moral values.'

Disheartened about all her plans Bonnie turned to a book for younger children, her attention caught by Maurice Sendak's *Where the Wild Things Are*, aimed at four to eight year olds, and a favourite of all her children in Reception class. The reasons given for its challenge were 'Because it depicted child abuse (a reference to Max not getting his supper)', and also that it was 'too dark and shows supernatural elements.'

Diary of a Wimpy Kid is banned for 'containing sexually explicit material, being obscene and being anti-friendly. The book is aimed at eight to twelve year olds. She found that six of the Dr Seuss books had been withdrawn from publication altogether since 2021. They were not banned but had been withdrawn by the company to avoid an embargo being introduced on all their titles. The lobby is so strong in the Republican states that you will now be hard pushed to find a copy of the six in order to form your own judgement. The statement from the company said they were withdrawn due to 'racist imagery'.

Being in the happy position of knowing that she would be walking away from this in three months when her husband's contract came to an end, she approached the school board and asked them for the justification. She wasn't confrontational, she just expressed an interest as it was different from at home, explaining that in the UK parents and, to a lesser extent, teachers decided what children read and what lessons they were taught from it.

To their credit a couple of the board looked uncomfortable, but the chair was a domineering character who, she would imagine, accepted no disagreement. He said it was so that children were not *'tainted';* did not grow up with the wrong ideas. Bonnie gently ventured that maybe to teach them to question logically would give them a more rounded view, but the meeting was pretty quickly closed down. There was no further discussion allowed.

The final straw for Bonnie was an article she read about one of the schools boards in Florida. This was January 2024, but read like something devised by the Puritans, or even from the dark ages.

The Board had withdrawn from its schools eight versions of the encyclopedia, five different versions of the dictionary, and all copies of the Book of Guinness World Records, as it is now called.

The reason given for these withdrawals? Students might look up words such as sex.

Her husband's brief tenure was completed in the USA in early 2024, and they caught the plane back to the UK. Bonnie had picked up a UK newspaper in the airport, and as they headed home she read an article that made her smile. Research in two USA universities, and informally supported by some School Boards and libraries, suggested that banning books for children in the USA was found to have increased the circulation of those books by 12%; exactly the opposite outcome to what the professionals were trying to achieve.

She was really happy to read this. Perhaps the madness of extremism was not going to win after all.

Bangers, No Mash

I suppose at the time it was logical that I blamed my sister. In later years I transferred that blame, rightly I now think, to my parents and the other adults who should have been adequately supervising the proceedings. I totally absolve my grandmother from all responsibility now as I did then. She was completely engrossed with toffee apples, baked potatoes and parkin in the kitchen. I can't help feeling that, had she been outside whilst the fireworks were being deployed, then things may have been different.

Even as I write my sister this absolution I am not sure. Several years older than me, she surely should have had more sense than to secure a banger horizontally in one of the gaps in my grandparents' dry-stone garden wall. How old was she? How old was I? I don't remember. Surely one of the adults there must have either lit the banger, or at least supervised her lighting it? I don't know.

What I do know is that the banger was lit, and being on the horizontal, it shot out of the wall across the path and hit me across the back of both of my knees. Looking back I think I must have been quite young for my knees to be no higher than the stones in that wall.

Whatever! I began to scream with the pain. I'm not sure I was even old enough to realise what was causing it, and I'm not sure I was old enough to have the words to explain why I was making a fuss. I remember getting told off for spoiling the bonfire party with my noise. I went indoors, to watch the fireworks through the dining room window, and I have hated bonfire night and fireworks ever since.

Once the celebrations were finished, the last firework extinguished, the toffee apples all eaten, I was taken upstairs for a bath. My misery had subsided to the occasional sob, but when put in the warm bathwater I screamed again. I can feel it now. Both knees, right across the crease at the back, where the banger had flown at full speed, hot and vicious.

'What on earth is the matter with you today? You're nothing but trouble.'

Then my mother began to towel me dry, and turning me round, saw the huge, angry burn blisters across both my knees, hidden earlier because of the creases that all children have there.

'Oh, you're hurt!'

Yes Mummy, I thought, *I've been trying to tell you that.*

It must be nearly seventy years now since that banger, although I still remember it. It'll be New Year's Eve in a few days, another excuse for fireworks. You'll find me tucked up in bed with the dog for company, the radio on and my book, waiting for it to be over for another year.

A Truly Delightful Gentleman

There are Centres of Excellence offering courses for students wanting to support deaf people and those suffering hearing loss, in just four universities across the UK. G had been fortunate enough to be offered a place at her first choice. It gave her a chance to shine. She thoroughly enjoyed the course and got on well with her fellow students.

Often, when a geographical area contains such a Centre of Excellence, it attracts individuals, charities and employers who have related interests. So for instance, in the city where G took up her university course, there is a range of support for BSL and Deaf Studies at undergrad and postgrad levels, and a significant deaf community has developed in the area. This includes a cohort of lecturers, interpreters and their families, many of the lecturers on the related courses being deaf themselves.

Also there are opportunities for research and development, such as hearing aid research and the area becomes established as one where related events are frequently held.

Soon after the start of her second year G and a friend volunteered as stewards for an event on campus, that was being sponsored by the British Deaf Association, and they duly turned up and supported those who were arriving at a strange city to feel more at home and access what they needed.

The keynote speaker was a gentleman I shall refer to as XX, who is well-renowned in the deaf community, both in the UK and the USA. He is a charismatic speaker who had published a book several years before through a UK publishing house. G had a copy of it already and brought it along for him to sign. He also had on sale his most recent textbook, this one published in the USA. G would have loved to have bought that, but as a student, funds wouldn't allow. Both she and her friend enjoyed the day though, and she spoke enthusiastically about it to the family.

On hearing the story G's Nan decided to do a bit of detective work, and duly contacted, by email, the charity who had organized the event. The reply she received to that initial enquiry basically pointed out that they were unable to help and because of Data Protection could not provide XX's details.

Fair enough! A more thoughtful approach was required and she put her thinking cap on. XX had worked with two publishing houses. Although it was the USA-published book that she wanted to buy, it seemed more logical to apply in the first instance to the publishers of his original book, as they were based in the UK.

The wording of the email to them needed careful thought, and she explained that she wanted to contact XX to buy a specially signed book, with G's upcoming twenty-first birthday in mind. She asked whether they could kindly make contact with him on her behalf.

The reply was almost immediate and very heartening:

'What a lovely idea. We regrettably can't supply you with contact details due to Data Protection. However we can certainly get in touch on your behalf. Should XX be happy to write a dedication, could I kindly ask for your granddaughter's name? We of course can't promise a positive response, but we'll try our best.'

'That is so kind of you. Her name is G and she will be 21 on (date). I really appreciate this.'

Within a few minutes there was another email from the publishing house, which was concerning. Such a prompt reply could surely only mean a rejection. The reality though could not have been more different:

'I've just heard back from XX, and he's actually perfectly happy for you to contact him. He's shared his email address for you (below) to make arrangements and said he could of course sign the book for you.'

The next email, sent to XX's e-mail address and outlining the situation, brought the following response:

'Many thanks for this lovely letter - ☺ Bless You. I would be delighted.'

I was warming to this gentleman. I could see why he had made such a positive impression on the students. The next part of his missive seemed quite apologetic:

'The book is £ (amount) and postage and packing £ (amount). I'm so sorry about the cost, but it is an American publisher and the book is heavy with 700+ pages. If you still want to go ahead I'll send you my bank details. Very best wishes, XX.'

'Dear XX, The price is absolutely fine and what I expected. If you get your bank details to me, I'll get my IT manager (hubby) on it ☺'

XX replied:

'Let me know whether you want me to draft an invoice, or do we just go ahead as you state above? An IT Manager! Oooh! I could do with one of those. Do you hire him out? The bank details are as follows ...'

'He'll sort it tomorrow for you and I'll let you know when the transfer has been made. Food for thought – hiring him out. ☺'

A couple of weeks later:

'Dear XX, Your book arrived this morning. Thank you so much for the lovely message for G. She will be thrilled – as am I. All the best,'

'Bless you, and keep well ☺, XX.'

The message inside G's book reads as follows:

'Happy 21st Birthday G, and wishing you the very best for your life, career and involvement with our deaf communities ☺, XX, 2023.'

After her birthday meal, at which Nan took a photograph of G's beaming smile as she read the inscription, and then looked across the table and grinned at her mother, she wrote one further email to XX:

'I won't bother you again, I promise. I just thought you might like to see G's face when she read the inscription in your book on her birthday.'

There was again a swift reply:

'You're not bothering me, I promise ;-) Thanks for sharing the photo and being lovely in general, XX, ☺'

What a truly delightful gentleman!

The Best Present

The time was right. The two young women shared a ground floor flat with outdoor space, and had long dreamed of getting their own dog. It was Jo who was really pushing for this, and they had established some ground rules. If asked, Jo would be hard put to define whether she and Danielle were second cousins, or first cousins once removed, but it was something like that. The point was that they got on well, and had agreed to the joint venture of being owned by a dog. The dog would be a rescue, and primary responsibility would lie with Jo. If, in the future the two went their separate ways, then Jo would keep the dog, with Danielle having visiting rights.

Millie looked like nothing more than a bag of bones when Jo and Danielle first saw her. It was at a rescue centre in the Welsh hills in January, and there had been snow overnight. The kennels for the rescue dogs were better than many they had seen, but they were still outdoor kennels, with a small enclosed area for sleeping. There were two dogs to each kennel, and Millie, to Jo's eyes, was easily the prettiest dog there, although she was painfully thin and a rather peculiar shape. She was tri-coloured, and the area around her eyes was jet black. The *Dusty Springfield* look they called it.

The kennels manager told them that he had tried to put weight on her over the two months since she was given up for rehoming, but the cold and the stress had got in the way of her wellbeing and she was still very underweight. At fourteen months she had not yet had a season, which for this breed usually happened well before the dog's first birthday, but he expected that as soon as she was settled then they could expect her to come on heat. It was often stress that delayed the normal course of events he told them.

They had a long journey home from the kennels when they collected Millie, and had factored into their planning that they would probably have to make frequent stops en route; they had no idea how well she would travel. Delightfully the reverse was true, and she slept for the full four hours of the journey. She must have been so exhausted after living outside with all those barking dogs for the two months since her initial owners had surrendered her to the rescue centre. Also the car was lovely and warm, and warmth was something she hadn't known during her December and January in the centre.

Jo worked from home, but at the time Danielle was working on a particularly tough project, which required a really early start each day. Jo's previous dogs, the same breed as Millie, had each happily slept overnight in a crate in the spare bedroom at her parents' house, and they had set up the smaller of the two crates ready for Millie's arrival. It was a disaster right from the start; as soon as Millie was coaxed into the crate – much against her will – she was shaking and crying, and once they left the room the howling began. They wondered whether she had slept her fill on the car journey, and hoped she would soon adjust to the new environment. But if anything it got worse. By the fifth night Danielle was tired and emotional. The dog's cries had escalated to what could only be described as screaming, and it went on all through each night, breaking off for a few minutes before starting up again with renewed vigour. Alarmed by Danielle's suggestion that Millie may have to go back, Jo phoned the rescue to see if she could find out more about Millie's life before she was given up for rehoming, and what was causing her so much distress.

The rescue manager told her that Millie had been acquired as a puppy by a married couple, both of whom worked full time. The man worked twelve hour shifts, and the woman worked a nine to five job an hour's commute from their home. This meant that sometimes they were both there with Millie, or one of them, but she was also left on her own for hours at a time, sometimes day after day. She had been given the run of the downstairs of their house, but was evidently bored and became destructive. Jo thought she'd be destructive too if she was on her own for hours. To stop the damage to their home they had started crating her when they were both out, hence her hatred of the crate. It also explained her disproportionately large shoulder muscles, which suggested that she had spent a lot of time trying to dig herself out of the crate.

Jo was in tears when Danielle came in from work. She wasn't sure which way to turn but Danielle had an idea.

'I know you've never done this, and your mum

would have a fit, but what do you think about taking Millie into your bedroom to sleep? We could put her new dog bed and some of her toys on the floor beside your bed, so she knows you're there. What do you think?'

It was certainly worth a try. That night they settled Millie into the dog bed, but within minutes she was on Jo's bed. Perhaps this was what she was used to. Presumably her first owners had needed their sleep too. She slept the night through, only moving around when Jo went to the bathroom, and snuggling up close again when she came back to bed.

Within two days of being allowed to sleep in comfort, the stress factor removed, Millie came on heat, her shape normalised as she put on weight, and she became a happy little girl, as long as she wasn't left.

It was some weeks later that Jo noticed some blood on the ground after Millie went out for a wee. It was very obvious on their white flagstones, and was very alarming. She had been checked over by the vet when she first came to them, but nothing had shown up. Now she had to visit the vet again, and undergo a general anaesthetic. Jo had been told to collect her at five o'clock and was alarmed to get a call at three.

'She's very vocal isn't she? We think she will continue to improve better at home. You can collect her at any time.' The receptionist sounded very desperate. Of course Millie would be in a crate, no doubt screaming her little head off and disturbing all the other recuperating patients, as well as all the staff.

'She's suffering from bladder stones,' was the verdict. Apparently similar to kidney stones, a build-up of calcium that lodges itself in the bladder. The stones will sometimes pass of their own accord, but, if large enough, will cause bleeding as the do. The solution was straightforward, a change to a medically prepared diet, and care about what treats she was offered.

There was just one more hurdle to overcome. Some people, no doubt with the best of intentions, feel it is okay to approach strange dogs, offering them food – usually biscuit based treats, exactly the worst thing for Millie to be given. There was one man in particular in the village, who would routinely do this on their morning walk, and one morning Jo was so upset she found herself shouting at this man that his supposed kindness was hurting her dog. It gave her pain and it made her bleed. Was that what he was trying to do? He had a dog of his own, for goodness' sake. Surely he could see why she was so angry. Especially as he then said, 'Oh, yes. You've told me this before.'

Jo's birthday came and there had been a few more meetings with this man that ended in Jo getting upset on Millie's behalf. Then she opened her birthday present from Danielle. It was brilliant; a short length of dog lead, red to match Millie's collar, and along it in white lettering was repeated: *Do not Feed*.

It worked. Each time she met the old man he would point to the lead and say, 'Do not Feed.' and no longer offered Millie anything more than a stroke and a cuddle.

For Jo the lead was the best present she could have received.

Acknowledgements

I firstly need to acknowledge the contribution of my daughter, whose interest in British Sign Language triggered the writing of this series of books.

Her interest was mirrored and built upon by her daughter Grace, who became interested to the extent of making BSL her future career and who is currently studying BSL and Deaf Studies at one of just four UK universities offering this as an undergraduate subject.

I want to thank members of the book club, Barbara, Clare, Freda, Gayle, Gill, Hilary, Jennifer, Kerry, Liz, Sue B, Sue R, and Sue S, who have tolerated being read to and who have commented, informing changes to some of the stories.

A particular mention goes to Clare, whose immediate response *'Oh Crumbs'* on hearing the initial outline of one of the stories, led to the title of the book.

Many thanks, as always, to Bowen's Book Publicity for wonderful promotional posts.

Notes

In writing these books of short stories I have gained some small insight into the world of deaf culture in the UK.

The story *20-20 Vision* in *The Hairdryer died Today*, about the deaf child on a plane journey, was written long before I had any other involvement with the deaf community. Before I published it, I spoke to my granddaughter Grace and she said that my first draft had failed to give an impression of what hard work it is being deaf, especially where there is loud ambient noise such as on a plane. We, as hearing people, are able to respond to a shout about safety, to our name being called to attract our attention, or to an announcement about maybe where we should be going next; to people who may be clapping their hands to get our attention. For deaf people, they have to be constantly watching, looking around to see whether anybody is trying to catch their attention or if there is anything they need to be aware of, and it is relentless.

Whereas there are approximately 179k – 250k words in English, there are 20k – 100k key signs that can be built into words in British sign language. To denote, for example, the difference between big and enormous, the sign language interpreter would also use body language and facial expressions.

Because a BSL interpreter has to get across the sense of what is being said at almost the same speed as normal speech, there is not time to build words individually letter by letter, unless an individual word is crucial to the understanding of the piece. That is why, when you watch sign language being interpreted, there is often a brief lapse after the speech starts so that the sense can be signed, rather than individual words.

Grace is studying BSL and Deaf Studies, and has 100% deaf lecturers, so there is always a translator in the room. Because the interpreters' work is such high intensity in that situation they work for 15 minutes, then have 15 minutes off, so there are two assigned to each class at any time, one on and one off.

Another thing I should have realised, but didn't, is that BSL evolves in the same way as English. My granddaughter went to Preston to university and found from the start that signs for some words or phrases were different from those she had encountered in Stoke. In the same way as English dialects vary according to where you are in the UK, so BSL too has its differences, and continues to evolve and change.

There are some areas where it is key to not just get across to a deaf person, the sense of what is being said, but the exact words that are being said, and to make sure that they understand them. For example if a deaf person is arrested and charged, any case could be challenged if they could demonstrate that they did not understand what they had been told. Similarly in a court situation, translators need to ensure that a defendant, their legal team, the opposing team, as well as a judge and maybe a jury, are all getting and understanding the same information.

Another example may be of a deaf individual learning to drive. It is crucial that a system is robust enough for them and the vehicle they are driving, to be safe from day one.

I have included this short section as these are things that intrigued me as I found out a little more about the culture of deaf communities. Now that BSL is being offered in a small but growing number of primary schools, and plans are in place from 2025 to introduce BSL as a GCSE subject, hopefully many more people will become competent at communicating through this method.

If you have enjoyed reading this and other books by Alison Lingwood, please leave feedback on amazon.co.uk